Tumbling

ILLINOIS SHORT FICTION

A list of books in the series appears at the end of this volume.

Kermit Moyer

Tumbling

UNIVERSITY OF ILLINOIS PRESS

Urbana and Chicago

Publication of this work was supported in part
by grants from the Illinois Arts Council, a state agency,
and the National Endowment for the Arts.

This book is printed on acid-free paper.

"In the Castle," *Sewanee Review,* 95 (Summer 1987)
"Tumbling," *Hudson Review,* 38 (Winter 1986)
"Life Jackets," *Crescent Review,* 4 (Fall 1986)
"The Compass of the Heart," *Georgia Review,* 37 (Fall 1983)
"Coming Unbalanced," *Southern Review,* 23 (Summer 1987)
"Ruth's Daughter," *Hudson Review,* 41 (Spring 1988)

Library of Congress Cataloging-in-Publication Data

Moyer, Kermit, 1943–
    Tumbling : stories / by Kermit Moyer.
        p.   cm.—(Illinois short fiction)
    ISBN 0-252-01525-8 (alk. paper)
    I. Title. II. Series.
PS3563.09365T86 1988
813'.54—dc19   87-34284
                                                CIP

to Amy

But tell me, who *are* they, these acrobats, even a little
more fleeting than we ourselves . . .

Rainer Maria Rilke
The Fifth Elegy

Contents

In the Castle

A little girl in a white nightdress is standing alone in the long upstairs hallway of an old beach hotel. The hallway is lit by a series of flared glass wall-fixtures that diffuse a warm, nearly amber light, and the hardwood floor is overlaid with a worn runner, so threadbare that its scenes of crinolined ladies and tailcoated gentlemen strolling in a park are barely discernible. On the faded wallpaper, columns of tiny pink-and-green roses alternate with sharp-edged vertical stripes of an indeterminate mauve. The girl is standing at a closed door beyond which voices are muffled but clearly audible. They're speaking another language, one she can't quite make out, a secret, charged language she's heard her parents use sometimes when they don't think she can hear. Reaching out her finger, she touches the door's lacquered, grain-whorled wood and feels a very slight, almost imperceptible, vibration. She stands that way for a moment, listening, and then, attracted by a flicker of light, looks down and notices a keyhole. Bending slightly, she puts her eye to the round opening above the slot and finds herself looking at a man and a woman she doesn't recognize. They're sitting at a table playing cards, and as the little girl watches, the man reaches across the table and slips his hand into the low-necked bodice of the woman's dress. Leaning forward into his touch and shrugging her shoulders as if to give his hand more room, the woman turns her head toward the door, and all at once the little girl is looking at the oval face of her mother, the same wide mouth, same hollows in the cheeks, the same black eyebrows she leaves unplucked. But the man is not the girl's father. Her father is clean-shaven, but this man has a mustache and a pointed beard just like her father's brother. He's dressed in a close-fitting seersucker suit and he looks as wiry and poised as a dancer. The girl's mother seems to be staring directly at her now, looking right through the keyhole, and the little girl pulls back from the door, turns away, and walks down the hallway to the stairs. She has found that by boosting herself up onto the banister she can look straight down the stairwell to the ground floor three stories below. The curved banister spirals round and round the stairwell, almost spinning, like the last of the bathwater going down the drain. She leans over, watching the way the lamplight slides on the polished wooden rail, thinking about that, not about her mother and her uncle John, recalling instead that she is really a princess magically imprisoned in this gigantic castle, her only friends the ordinary things that surround her, the secretly animate furniture, stoic ashtrays, the wise old newel post standing there beside her on the landing. Everything has been frozen in place by a magic spell. But if she can break the spell, all her furniture friends will come unfrozen, they'll all move and dance once again and the world will be filled with their happy, singing voices. To show her appreciation, and her gratitude for their devotion, the little girl determines to stroke her hand gently down the whole length of the friendly stairwell banister, from the newel post at the head of the stairs all the way down to the curled paw at the bottom. Humming to herself a special magic song, the little girl carefully lifts the train of her nightgown with one hand, cups the smooth wood of the rail with her other, and is about to start down the stairs when suddenly the elevator's antique doors rattle and slide open. She stops and turns just as her father steps out of the elevator into the hall. "Why, hello," he says in a surprised voice. "Aren't you supposed to be in bed?" The little girl looks down at the floor, as if she expects a scolding, but her father only shakes his head and laughs. "What are little girls made of?" he asks in the voice he gets when he's been drinking. "Sugar 'n' spice 'n' everything nice," the little girl answers, lifting her head and smiling. Now her father takes her hand and together they walk down the hallway to another door, one that's been left slightly ajar. Her father pushes it open and they enter a room exactly like the other one. Here, too, there's a table and a deck of cards. "Your mother must still be saying good-night," her father tells her, and then, indicating the cards, "Sit down. I'll teach you a new game while we wait." Obediently, the little girl takes a chair opposite her father, and he shows her a game in which each has to lay down and pick up and then lay down again. The game goes on and on, the only sounds the ticking of the pendulum clock on the wall and the quiet snapping of the cards, clubs and diamonds, hearts and spades. The little girl draws card after card, until at last the door opens and in comes her mother. She's sleek in a long satin gown, and she's humming a song to herself, the way she often does. She goes to a mirror just inside the door and reaches up to unpin her hair. The little girl turns in time to see the thick brown curls come tumbling undone around her mother's shoulders. "Who's winning?" her mother asks, adjusting her bodice and yawning. A faint scent of flowers and musk floats in on a current of stirred-up air. "I am," the little girl lies, turning back to her hand and discarding. "She'll be beating you before long," her father adds, giving the little girl a wink.

* * *

The next afternoon, while her mother and father are napping, the little girl's uncle John takes her for a stroll on the boardwalk. He wears a straw hat with a rolled brim and carries a thin, mottled cane that is tapered and jointed like a long, skinny finger. Before they start out, he snaps open the lid of his gold pocket watch and studies the dial as if he were consulting a compass. "Just breathe that salt air," he says, as they step from the dusk of the hotel lobby out into the dazzling brilliance of the afternoon. Great, pillowy clouds drift just above the ocean's horizon, and fearing that she too might float away, the little girl takes hold of her uncle John's hand and makes sure, as she walks along beside him, always to keep one foot planted firmly on the ground. The palm of her uncle John's hand is moist, and his fingers are as plump as the sausages they ate that morning for breakfast—she and her father, her mother and Uncle John, sitting together at a round table with white linen napkins of a startling crispness tented over their thighs. The sausages were so juicy they squirted every time she took a bite, and now, as she imagines poking one of her uncle John's fingers into the mustard bowl, the little girl tosses her head and giggles, accidently brushing her cheek against the pin-striped sleeve of her uncle John's seersucker jacket. The cloth has such a soft, crinkly texture that she closes her eyes and brushes her cheek against it again. "You like that, do you?" her uncle John says. "Do you want to know a secret?" He bends down to her level and when he whispers in her ear his breath makes a tickle. "Buzz, buzz, buzz," he tells her, giving her a hug, and then, "That's what *I* say—*you* say, 'Fuzzy, fuzz, fuzz.' " And he tilts his head toward her, bending down so close that the little girl can see tiny hairs on the pendulous lobe of his ear. Obediently, she raises up her lips, giggles because the words after all are so silly, and whispers exactly what she has been told, secretly unsurprised when the touch of her breath causes her uncle John to give a funny little shiver.

* * *

That night, just as the little girl is on the verge of sleep, the moon comes to the open window beside her hotel bed and calls to her. The moon's voice is an intermittent sigh, or a moan, audible just under the hushing sound of the surf. The little girl pulls back her sheet and slides down from her high bed to the cool, moonlit floor. Holding her breath and stepping toward the window, she wades out until the moonlight is well over her head. The moon's face, suspended low in the clear night sky, is pale and perfectly round: it's the face of a beautiful, light-filled woman who is the little girl's secret friend. The moon smiles at the little girl for answering her call, and when she whispers, her breath is as fragrant as oranges or a freshly split melon: "Look," the moon sighs, "look there at your father." And the little girl lowers her eyes to where the breaking surf streaks the black ocean. The surf is as white as the sand, and on the sand there are shadows as black as the ocean. Out of one of these, a man appears, a man the little girl is sure can't be her father. Standing naked in the moonlight, he glistens like a fish, and as the little girl watches, he crosses the beach, wades awkwardly out, and throws himself headlong into the silvery net the moon has fashioned with her hair and spread out over the water. Instead of getting tangled, the man climbs the net like a ladder, hand over hand, fin over fin, making his way toward where the moon's wide mouth yawns open. "You won't really eat him?" says the little girl to the moon. "Oh, but we must," laughs the moon. "It's how we make the stars. And, besides, it's not really eating." But to the little girl's horror—and secret delight, since she knows he isn't really her father—the man climbs headfirst into the mouth of the moon and disappears entirely.

* * *

The next morning, the little girl wakes with a yawn, rubs the sand from her eyes, and stretches. Her father is standing next to the bed. Sunlight streams in through the window behind him, so his face is in shadow, but she can smell the peppery scent of his cologne over the other smell of tobacco. Relieved to find that he hasn't been swallowed up after all, the little girl reaches out and gives him a great big hug, nestling her head against his vest just above the gold watch chain that hangs across the soft bulge of his belly. "Oh, Daddy," she tells him, "I thought you turned into a fish." "Shhh!" her father whispers, putting a finger to his lips. "I used to be a fish, but I converted." When he chuckles, his stomach quivers against the little girl's cheek. "Aren't you up yet?" her mother calls from the doorway. "Breakfast has already started." Her mother is wearing a pink silk dressing gown and combing her hair with one of the little girl's secretly animate friends, a lovely, long-toothed tortoiseshell comb whose husband is a matching brush with stiff black bristles. "Is Uncle John coming?" asks the little girl. "Of course he's coming—he always comes," her mother answers, and as she finishes a downstroke and raises the comb for another, a few fine tendrils of hair float up into the light, following after the tortoiseshell comb as though they simply can't get enough of her. "Fuzzy, fuzz, fuzz," the little girl sings to herself, pulling her yellow pinafore over her head and turning so her father can do up the back buttons. "Oh, I know that one," her father tells her: *"Fuzzy Wuzzy was a bear. Fuzzy Wuzzy had no hair. Fuzzy Wuzzy wasn't fuzzy, was he?"* And at the end of the rhyme, he tickles a finger up the little girl's spine, a trick she's seen him play on her mother, and the little girl lets out a squeal of delight, shivering all over with a sudden rash of goose bumps. "There's your uncle John at the door," her mother says, repositioning the shoulder strap of her brassiere. "Hush, now, and try to act like a lady."

* * *

After a wonderful breakfast of applesauce pancakes and syrup, the little girl follows her parents and her uncle John out through the French doors of the dining room onto a wide gallery that faces the sea. The four of them stand in a row at the wooden balustrade, look at purple clouds massing on the horizon like the swelled breasts of a flock of giant pigeons, and try to gauge the weather. "I'm afraid we're in for a nasty morning," the little girl's uncle John says. "Perhaps we'd better go back to bed." He slides a cigar from the cylindrical silver container he keeps in his left breast pocket, snips off the end with a tiny pair of scissors, rolls the cigar around in his mouth, licking it as if it were the flap of an envelope he's sealing, then draws back his lips and clenches it between his teeth. "I wouldn't mind a round of Hearts," the little girl's mother says. "I know how to play Hearts, too," sings out the little girl, watching her uncle John rotate the tip of his cigar over the flame of his silver lighter. "Daddy showed me how to shoot the moon." "No, no, no," says her father. "That was to be a surprise. Remember?" Moodily, the little girl lowers her chin to the weathered old balustrade—a steadfast friend who supports her and who would no doubt counsel her, too, if he weren't under a spell—and gazes out at the ocean, which has darkened to the color of an overripe plum. "There, now," says the little girl's mother, gently stroking her hair. "If you're going to shoot the moon, the last thing you want to do is tell." Uncle John takes the cigar from his mouth, exhales a gray plume of smoke, and says in an explanatory way, "The child merely said she knows how the game is played—and I dare say she does." He reaches out and chucks the little girl under the chin. "Isn't that right?" he says, and when she looks up at him and nods, he rolls the cigar between his lips, puffing on it so that its ruby-red eye gleams at her and winks.

* * *

Gusts of rain are pulsing against the window panes when the little girl wakes up from her nap. Her father lies sleeping beside her, his face obscured by the arm he's flung over his head. His vest gapes open around the loosened tongue of his tie, but otherwise he's fully dressed. He's even wearing his shoes. After drinking a bottle of wine during lunch, he sleeps like someone under a spell. Nevertheless, the little girl slips down from the bed as quietly as she can and tiptoes into the sitting room. Except for the clock ticking on the wall and the rattling sound of the rain, the hotel is perfectly still. Now, as happens sometimes when it's quiet and there's no one else around, the little girl's furniture friends—the upholstered wing chair in the corner, the wooden hat stand by the door, the brass lamp in the middle of the drop-leaf table—seem to turn subtly toward her and, imminent with secret life, to teeter on the verge of some marvelous change. Moment by moment the pressure builds until finally, unable to stand any more of it, the little girl goes to the door and, still barefoot and dressed only in underclothes, releases herself into the hallway. She's humming her special song to herself and running her finger along the wall, passing over row after row of pink-and-green roses with never a thorn to harm her, when suddenly a door opens and out come Uncle John and her mother. He's leaning over her mother's shoulder, whispering something into her ear, and both of them are laughing. Quickly, the little girl makes herself invisible by fixing her eyes on the worn hallway runner, where a lady carrying a parasol walks arm in arm with a gentleman in a top hat while two deep-chested greyhounds prance among the trees beside them. And as the little girl stares at the carpet, she sees that one of the tapestried greyhounds is in fact a living, breathing toad. Its colors blend in with the colors of the carpet, but the bumps on its skin are all shiny, and its eyes are like great green marbles with spirals of amber inside them.

*   *   *

"I know a secret," the little girl says to her father. It's after dinner and the two of them are out on the hotel's gallery sitting side by side facing the sea. "Be careful," says the little girl's father. "Sometimes when you tell a secret, it turns into a kangaroo." "Oh, Daddy," laughs the little girl. The sun has already gone down, and the moon, no longer quite full, is floating in a sky streaked with scarlet and violet. "Then it jumps up and down and thumps its fat tail," says her father. "Like this?" says the little girl, drumming her palms against the arms of her chair. "Exactly," says her father, and as he drains the last of the amber liquid from the tall glass in his hand, the ice cubes shift with a sound like the links of a gold chain falling gently together. "But it's not *my* secret," the little girl explains. "It's a secret of the *moon's*." "Ah," says her father. "I see. Well, you can't very well give away what's not yours. Go ahead, then, let's have it." The little girl stares wide-eyed at where the moon's face seems to have turned slightly away from them out toward the sea, and then whispers: "The moon told me the stars are her babies." "Well, well," says her father. "And I always thought the moon laid great clusters of eggs—like a toad." "Oh, Daddy," the little girl says with a shudder, her shoulders scrunching up and shivering at the very idea.

*   *   *

The moon has sunk well beneath the dark edge of the ocean, leaving only the stars to enlighten the sky, when the little girl awakens and looks up from her pillow. Crouching on the porcelain chamber pot, all awash with starlight in the far corner there next to the washstand, is the same great, glistening toad. In the glimmering light of the stars, the toad's encrusted skin glitters like emeralds and rubies. Half-lidded and sleepy, his protuberant eyes glow with the knowledge of dreams, and his veined throat, swollen to twice the size of his head, pulses in time with the little girl's breathing. The long slit of his crocodile mouth is just curving into a smile when the little girl's mother drifts into the room from the doorway. As if she's been beckoned, she glides across the floor to the chamber pot in the corner, turns, lifts her nightgown's billowing white skirt, and squats over the porcelain pot with a sigh, letting the gown settle back down like a curtain. And after a while, when she arises, smiling, there's not one trace of the toad.

*   *   *

The next day, kneeling on the beach in her swimming suit, the little girl is casting a tower for her sand castle with a small tin pail. After she has packed the pail firmly, she inverts it over the nearest of the castle's many corners, adjusts the pail's position, and then, lifting it ever so gently, reveals, as if by magic, a perfectly tapered cylinder of sand. The castle rises like a wedding cake in three narrowing tiers and is ornamented with an intricate system of crenellated parapets that connect its various turrets and towers. The little girl has been working all afternoon. When she started, the farthest reach of the surf seemed a long way away, but now it licks at her heels as she squats in the sand and she begins to feel an impulse to hurry. Using the pail as a scoop, she digs a moat all round the castle, making it so deep that for a time, as the afternoon wanes and the flood tide advances, the moat succeeds in diverting the water. But at last, despite all her efforts, the bottom edge of the castle begins to erode and crumble. Soon, the water is up to her ankles—it submerges the moat and surrounds the castle entirely. Backing away from the surf into the cool of the hotel's long shadow, the little girl looks up, to rest her attention, and watches sea gulls, their wings dark-tipped and tilted, bank and glide over the shallows, squawking and searching for dinner. She feels a pressure in her bladder and, looking down at her sand castle, sees that from this angle it appears to crouch there in the water like a gigantic toad. At this very moment, in the great castle behind her, all her furniture friends are poised, she can feel it, teetering on the very edge of some magical transformation. Her father is probably sleeping, and her mother and Uncle John are no doubt playing Hearts, the stiff cards snapping— clubs and diamonds, hearts and spades—as they are laid down and picked up and laid down again, her mother and Uncle John each shooting the moon in succession. Above the ocean's horizon, the moon itself is so pale it could be a whisper.

Tumbling

Early one rainy morning just about a week ago, Jack and me were sitting in a laundromat in this little town where we'd spent the night in an unlocked car. We sleep in cars a lot of times, it's not as bad as you might think. A little cramped maybe, but if there's a radio and a key to make it work, we don't mind too much. Like that night we were in a big new-smelling Cadillac in a used-car lot. Jack said they could make it smell that way with an aerosol can. Plenty of room and everything clean and shiny. The radio picked up stations from as far away as Chicago and Fort Wayne, Indiana, and we sang along with the top forty and listened to one of those shows where people call in. Jacky tried to get a station from back home to see if there was anything on about us, but he couldn't find one. He said the signals were probably too weak to reach as far as we were by then. He was sitting behind the wheel smoking Camels because it was Daddy's brand. I hated for him to get that clean ashtray dirty. I don't know why. I said we should think of the folks that might want to buy that car. Jack just laughed and said maybe a few cigarette butts might give them a chance to think about us. "But wouldn't that be leaving evidence?" I said. That's one of the things Jacky talks about sometimes: covering our tracks, he calls it. He wipes our fingerprints off the radio knobs and the steering wheels, and he's always careful to use a handkerchief to open and close the doors. Well, that morning dawned so rainy-gray and drizzly you didn't even want to move. Jacky let me sleep with the duffel bag for a pillow and I just rolled myself up with my hands pressed between my knees and tried to keep what was happening in my dream from slipping away. It was a birthday party and it was you, Mom, not Jacky, helping me blow out the candles. I was wearing my blue print dress with the puffy sleeves and the white lace collar, and Jacky was saying, "Let me, let me." There was pink icing on the cake and I wanted to see if maybe Daddy was there too. I thought he might be because we were still little in my dream. But Jack was shaking my shoulder and telling me to rise and shine, we had to get out of there before they opened up. So I combed my hair in the rearview mirror, and then we scooted out and found this laundromat, which was either already open or else hadn't ever closed. We were wet from the rain by that time, so we got behind the machines and changed into some dry clothes. We put a wash in and then just sat around, watching the raindrops slide down the windows and reading magazines. We had the place all to ourselves, and it made me feel kind of blue, looking out at nothing but the rain and two or three parked cars. There was a Woolworth's right across the street that hadn't opened up yet. It was only about six o'clock in the morning. I could see a BACK TO SCHOOL sign in one window and I wondered if come September we'd be going back to school or not. My dream was still with me, too, but all scattered and floating away from where it came from. A foggy picture would come in front of my mind's eye, and I'd think it was something I was about to remember, something that really happened, and then I'd realize it was only my dream, and that'd make me feel like I'd lost something. The fat sound of the washer going chugga-*whoosh*-chugga-*whoosh* and the little pinging noise of the dryer had put me into sort of a hypnotic trance anyway. But not Jacky. He was reading a *Time* magazine, making noises to himself whenever he'd find something interesting. "Hey, listen to this," he says. "Remember what I told you? *Scientists now believe that the universe has been expanding from a single fixed point for millions of years. If we trace back the motion of the galaxies, we arrive at a point in the distant past when they were a single unified mass, a time when the universe must have been very different from its present disseminated state.*" I turned away from the window and said, "What do you mean, 'remember what I told you'? I don't remember anything like that." "Come on, Jill," he says, "everything's always moving away, I always said that, and we're going against the current anytime we try to keep them, you know, from flying apart, or anytime we try to get them back together again. That's why

it's so hard, and that's why we have to be so careful all the time." "Oh,
yeah," I said. "Sure. We're just like the galaxies."

It was right then that this big fat lady comes into the laundromat. She's
got a whole wicker basket full of dirty laundry, so she pushes the door
open with her shoulder and sort of backs in. When she turns around
and sees us she flinches. "Land sakes," she says. "You give me a
fright. I never expected a soul in here this early." Her face was one of
those bright lit-up country kind with rosy apple cheeks—made red
from bunches of tiny little broken veins I saw later—a face just as shiny
wet from the rain as if she'd been crying her eyes out, except she
looked so pleased with everything you couldn't believe she'd even
know how to cry. She had round arms with freckles and her hair was
just like yours, Mom—reddish strawberry-blonde—all twisted up in
braids at the back of her head and against her neck. I was glad she was
here because now I thought maybe I could get out of feeling so blue.
Jacky'd be sure to put on one of his shows, and that meant I'd have
to play along. Which usually I get a kick out of. Anytime we talk to
somebody I have to wait and see who we're going to be this time. Real
life is always so ordinary on the one hand and so complicated on the
other, but Jacky's stories can make it all seem just as simple and easy
as filling in a coloring book. "Can you tell us about how far we are
from the Maryland line?" he says. The fat lady is still standing there
with her arms hooped around this big basket of laundry. Jacky's got
that funny way of being able to get your attention, and I could see her
sort of tilt her head like she's having trouble hearing what he's trying to
tell her. She says, "Not far—only about fifty miles, I guess. Just take
Route 15 south out of town. Do you all have family in Maryland?"
Jacky looks up at her and directly into her eyes. He sort of waves his
hand over toward me and says, "This is Peggy Sue." *Peggy Sue?* I
thought. He's got to be kidding. I just sat there with my hands folded in
my lap and looked sort of lost—which was easy enough because that's
just exactly how I felt, we'd been on the road almost two weeks by
then, sticking to the back roads. In a way I was in the same boat as the
fat lady, just waiting to find out what the story would be so I could play
along. So then Jack says, "We're on our way to Maryland to get mar-

ried." I closed my eyes for a second and tried to take that one in. When
I looked up, the fat lady is staring at me and resting her basket on the
formica table between the row of washers on one side and the row of
dryers on the other. "Why, you're just kids," she says. If I turned
slightly toward the window, I could see my reflection in the glass. It
was all wavery from the rain. "Just a couple of kids," she says. I'm
watching her in the reflection on the window and I can see right
through her to the five-and-ten across the street. "You don't want to
hear any of this," Jacky says. He's staring down at his hands and
shaking his head back and forth. I can see him in the window too—our
reflections have a sharp edge to them but the raindrops, sliding crooked
down the glass, make everything outside blurry. "Look here," she says
out of the blue, her head tilted and her voice going all kindly and soft.
"You're in a family way, isn't that right child?" When I turned around
she was watching me with a sly, sort of happy look. Jacky sits up
straight, like he's suddenly got everything under control. "We're all
right. We can take care of ourselves," he says. The fat lady's watching
Jacky again, and she narrows her eyes and says, "How old are you
kids? Where're you from?" "We're old enough, you don't have to
worry about that," Jacky says right away. Then he says, "At least we're
old enough in Maryland—we're just passing through here." He got that
line from a movie we'd seen where somebody had to go to Maryland to
get married because they were underage. We go to movies a lot on the
road, for the simple reason that movie theaters turned out to be a good
place to spend the night. "What about you?" she says to me. "Are you
old enough too?" I circled my arms around my stomach and said, "It
looks like I am." The fat lady nods her head and turns back to Jacky.
"Well then I guess you better get yourselves a map the next time you
fill up," she says. For a second it looked like that was the end of the
conversation, but then Jacky says, "We're not driving, we don't have a
car." He stops short, and then he blurts out, "We've been hitchhiking."
Which was true enough, that's for sure—one of the problems is being
too young to have a driver's license much less a car. All we have is the
money we got from cashing Daddy's check—which I'm real sorry
about, Mom, but Jacky made out a good case it was his and mine in the
first place. And we decided, or rather I should say he did, that we'd

pretty much have to forget about riding on buses or trains or anything like that because otherwise we'd be sure to get picked up. So there we were sitting in a laundromat at six in the morning. For some reason, I remember, I kept listening to the rain. The light in that laundromat was real yellow against all the gray outside, and since this fat lady came in, the sound of the rain made it, I don't know, sort of cozy and warm-feeling somehow. "So you'll be looking for a ride then I guess," she says to Jacky. "I want you to know I think you're doing the right thing. I know it's bound to be hard for a spell, but you'll be just fine if you really love one another." She smiles in a way that makes it hard not to believe her. I immediately started to brighten up. Then she says, "Are you hungry, have you two had any breakfast yet? You must be starved." I felt like we were turning a corner when she said that. I don't know why, except it made me think of you asking that same question the time you didn't get back from your date until early Sunday morning and we were already up. You were still dressed fancy from Saturday night and you tried to tell us you'd been to church already. I could just see you in that navy blue cocktail dress with the bow at the bust whipping up jelly omelets and French toast and once in a while tossing your hair out of your eyes the way you do when your hands are full. Standing by the stove in your stocking feet after you'd kicked off your heels. Remembering that made me feel like a little kid, and here I was supposed to be pregnant and everything. When we don't answer her, the fat lady looks at Jack and tells him, "You need to make sure this girl eats on a regular schedule. She's a little lady now, and she'll have to keep her strength up." Then she turns to me and says, "Don't worry, I wouldn't tell your secret to a soul, but you'll have to eat enough for the baby too, that's the first thing." She smiled and I nodded and she says, "Good. Now just let me get this wash started. Our dryer's all right, but the Bendix's been on the fritz, so here I am. Well. We'll have to see about getting some nourishment into you. It's not healthy to be as skinny as you are in your condition." To tell the truth, I *was* just about starved, and I was also glad to let this fat lady take charge for a while—even if it was under false pretenses. I was avoiding Jacky's eyes because I didn't want to be reminded of that at all. I just wanted to be taken care of for a little while. Maybe I'd even get to take a bath. In my dream there were lots and lots of candles on the cake even though we were little, and when I couldn't blow them all out you blew out the rest, so I knew all my wishes were going to come true. Jacky was crying and he kept saying, "Let me, let me," but that didn't really matter. The feeling I had in my dream was this: I didn't know what my wishes were, but I just had a feeling they were all going to come true.

I think it was something about the fat lady herself that made Jack come up with that particular story. The trick Jacky has is he can pretty much hook up the right story with the right person. He just lets them make it up with him. That's where the fat lady was a natural. She really loved the idea of us running off because we had to get married. It might be a speck scandalous, she said, but that's all right, these things always happened this way. She expected we'd be as happy as anybody else and, besides, the baby was a sure sign. So now I had to play my part in this hot teenage romance she and Jack cooked up. Star-struck lovers and everything. And that's probably right where it all started, from then on it's just been one thing after another. Like running off to find Daddy in the first place. If you look at it from a distance, I guess it's pretty ridiculous. But each step of the way it seemed perfectly natural and, the funny thing is, after a while the reasons why hardly seemed to matter. I knew you'd be worried about us, but I also knew you'd be all right and I wasn't so sure about Jacky. And anyway at first I thought I'd be able to steer him home before you even got back from your weekend in the city. But the plan of how to do each step of the thing somehow took over. Each step always makes sense—even if the whole thing doesn't. Daddy's supposed to be in Brunswick, Georgia, so that's where we're going. And of course running off was a good way to make you feel sorry too. Jacky's sure you spent the weekend with that guy from work, the one that brought you home after the office party. I guess you never knew it, but Jacky saw the two of you kissing or something in the kitchen that night. Those things don't matter to me, but where you're concerned Jacky can't even stand the idea of stuff like that. So going off to find Daddy was a bright light for Jacky—he *had* to follow it. And I just had to go along. I guess I've always felt like I had to look after Jacky, even if he is eight minutes older than me. I don't only mean take care of him exactly—I mean more like I have to follow him with my mind and with my feelings. He gets so worked up about stuff sometimes, and really, things like that just never mattered to me. What's actually happening matters a lot more than anything you might merely think about it, don't you agree?

You should have seen the fat lady's house. But of course she wasn't the fat lady by then. We found out her name was Mrs. Spicer, and she had a whole flock of kids, most of them grown now, and grandchildren—the youngest was only about four years old. Well, it didn't take long before Jack had Mrs. Spicer eating out of his hand. He'd tease her and make her laugh and pretty soon she's treating him like he's her favorite son or something. But I don't think she ever pictured me as one of her daughters though. I was more like somebody she used to be herself, that's what she told me. We got in the front seat of this Chevrolet station wagon she had, and then she drove us just barely outside of town to a big old pink house with blue shutters and lots of peaks and chimneys and three wide porches, a screened one up on the second floor just for sleeping—all of it set back on a low hill you couldn't even see from the highway because of all the trees. Everything surrounded by cornfields and peach orchards and a flower garden big enough to walk through, almost like a little park. Just to get there you had to go up a long driveway, really an actual road, between tall rows of ever-green trees. We weren't that far from the mountains—Jacky'd pointed them out from the road, and I'd already felt the temperature drop. He showed me on the map how close we were to where the color changed from yellow to long fingers of brown. Those were the Blue Ridge Mountains, he said. One of Jacky's ideas was to take the Appalachian Trail down to Georgia. Brunswick's over on the coast though, about an inch-and-a-half down from Savannah. According to the mileage chart, an inch-and-a-half is about seventy-five miles. Jacky kept changing his mind between going through the mountains and then cutting east along what he called "Sherman's march to the sea" or going along the coast through all the Navy bases and ocean cities as we made our way down to Brunswick. It was a hard decision, and we were right at the turning point that day. He liked to read out the names of the towns and cities between here and there, saying them over while he moved his fingertip along the different paths: Winchester or Norfolk? Asheville or

Southport? Atlanta or Charleston, South Carolina? Jacky always pays
attention to the names of places. To Jacky it's like the name of each
little town we come to—especially if they have funny ones like Buffalo
Mills or Mann's Choice or Rainsburg, Pennsylvania—like each little
town is his to put away and keep, or like us just knowing the names of
those places is what's making them come true. That's why I thought we
might end up going east after all: there's just more names in that direction, and going off toward the blue edge of the map seemed more
definite to Jacky than just trailing down through the mountains, I could
tell. I was sure hoping so anyway, even though I never imagined for a
minute we'd find Daddy either way. I just figured if we stayed close to
people we'd be okay, but if we went off into the woods who knows
what might happen? We don't even have sleeping bags, just a worn-out
Navy blanket and that ratty old wedding-ring quilt you remember was
my favorite. I like woods and open country, but what I like best is
coming into a town, seeing the billboards, passing the first house with
a painted fence and a mowed lawn, then maybe coming to an Esso
station and a Dairy Queen. We'd always stop for one of those ice-cream
cones with a curl-on-the-top, and Jacky'd already be studying the map,
looking for the crookedest line between this town and the next one and
licking away at the mustache of vanilla on his upper lip.

We stayed with Mrs. Spicer for two entire days, and during the whole
time Jack was Buddy and I was Peggy Sue. That's one of our favorite
songs, "Peggy Sue," and those names were sort of a secret joke to
Jacky. He especially liked it that Mrs. Spicer probably never even
heard of that record or of Buddy Holly either (which I found out later
she had, on her own radio). I keep hearing that song in my mind
because of those names—*I love you, Peggy Sue, with a love so rare and
true, uh-oh Peg-gy, my Peg-gy Sue-uh-ooo, uh-ooo-ooo.* That's what I
mean about the way Jacky can always get you to thinking exactly what
he wants. I mean it was fine with me, that's what we'd been doing all
along anyway—and it's fun too, always acting out some story or other.
Jack says we have to stay incognito because we can never be sure if
anyone's after us or not. We're runaways, he says, and it's safer to keep
changing identities. Sometimes I'm his sister and other times I'm not—

sometimes I'm his sidekick or his leading lady. But there's always some story going along with it. Even looking for Daddy. That's real, I guess, I mean that's something we're *doing,* but it's really just another story too. The stuff that actually happens, day by day, that stuff doesn't have anything to do with Daddy. Like Mrs. Spicer. Can you feature her taking us into her bedroom to ask us about our "hygiene practices"? That's what she called it. She said we were right to leave such things up to God Almighty. She said she thanked the Lord for all of her children. She wasn't a heathen and she could see we weren't either. "Oh, yes, ma'am," Jacky says, looking over at me sort of moony. "Our love is holy, we know that." Mrs. Spicer just widens her eyes and says, "Amen."

After we got to her house that first morning, she fixed us some corn fritters—these little things like pancakes with whole kernels of corn in them—all we could possibly eat—along with thick country sausage and a big round blue pitcher of milk. We always use the carton at home, so I remember that pitcher, round as a peony and with a kind of pinched-in spout like a flower petal. It was the sort of thing anybody'd love to have themselves someday—that house too, lots of nooks and crannies, so perfectly homey you could hardly believe it, little touches like em-broidered cushions on the window seats of these bay windows at all the stairway landings—I bet the house Jacky and me are staying in right now used to be a lot like that, except this one's falling apart and there's no furniture to speak of, only this broken-down rocking chair I'm sit-ting in and what we managed to pull together out of cardboard boxes and some old wooden milk crates Jack found in the cellar. But I'm sure this used to be a really fabulous mansion though, back in the Gay Nineties or the Roaring Twenties or whatever. We're right next to the ocean, I can hear the surf against the stone wall across the road this very minute. Maryland, or maybe Delaware, I think. It's hard to know exactly which state you're in where we are now.

You might have liked Mrs. Spicer, she was wonderful in a lot of ways, but I doubt that you would have. You don't like anybody sitting in judgment all the time, no matter how kindly they try to tell you what you're doing wrong. I'm like you, my feeling is: whatever anybody else says, I've got my own reasons. But even if Mrs. Spicer could get on your nerves a little bit, you still had to hand it to her. Picture this: the three of us're sitting in this big old country kitchen—four long windows looking out on a vegetable garden where you can see bulging red tomatoes in chicken-wire cages and leafy, purple-colored cabbages. Copper pots and pans are hanging on the wall, and there's this great stone fireplace. The kitchen table's covered with a bright blue-check oilcoth. We're just finishing breakfast and Jack's drinking a cup of coffee—which he taught himself to like after we went on the road, the same with smoking. It goes along with his idea of how he ought to be. So Jacky's drinking his coffee, and Mrs. Spicer's over at the sink looking through the window at something outside. She leans up against the rim of the sink and raps on the middle part of the window—it's open at both the top and the bottom—and she calls out through the screen, "Here, Wendell, you better let sleeping dogs lie—old Bertha's not going to like that. Why don't you and William go on over to your tree house and read some comic books?" Over her shoulder she says, "William's from down the road, he just got a new tricycle." Then through the screen she calls, "You heard me now, you better not tease Bertha like that—" and from over on the other side of the kitchen, farthest from the sink, a deep voice pipes in: "Oh, Mama, let 'em be. A little scrimmage with Bertha might do 'em good." When I turned around to see who's here now, I notice Jacky's still got his eye on Mrs. Spicer. Before he looks he's waiting to see what her reaction's going to be, just as crafty as a fox. I figured whoever's in the doorway's probably Mister Spicer, which it turned out he was, only not Mister but Major. I'm just trying to kind of slide a glance by him, I don't want to give anything away, but he locks onto my eyes, bang, and gives me a big wink—like we know a secret that makes everybody else look like fools, or like he's telling me this fat lady's harmless so we might as well play along. When I look back down at my plate, I see there's only a stub of fried sausage left—which I stick with my fork and smear around in the maple syrup before putting it in my mouth. Mrs. Spicer was a great cook, you'd have thought so too—that sausage was probably the best I ever had, and the corn fritters were entirely out of this world. We'd been pretty much living on french fries and popcorn and Coke for days by then. I'm starting to pour myself some more milk from the blue pitcher, when

Jacky stands up and says, "Good morning, sir!"—like a military cadet or something. That's exactly how long it took Jacky to figure him out. "At ease, son, at ease," the guy says. "Sit down and finish your coffee. And you, young lady," he says to me, "you must be little sister, is that right?" I smiled and shook my head and waited for Jack to explain our story, but he never had to—Mrs. Spicer charges right in and does it for him, all in one breath nearly, leaving out the part about me being pregnant, and finishing up with, "So I thought you might take them down to Hagerstown on Saturday when you and Sam Healey go in to the races." Then she turns toward us and says, "This is my husband, Major Spicer." "Pleased to meet you, sir," Jacky chimes in right away, offering his hand. I said, "Same here," and gave him back a wink of my own. I don't know why. I guess I thought at least the two of us might have our feet on the ground, even if nobody else did.

It turned out I was wrong about that—was I ever—but the guy did give you the impression of being absolutely no-nonsense and in-charge—very distinguished looking, but with this crinkly little smile around the edges that seemed to bring him right down to earth and make it sort of a joke that anybody of our intelligence, his and mine I mean, would actually have to tolerate the kind of foolishness we had to put up with. I mean you felt like he was including you in the winner's circle with him—at least that's how he made me feel. And then the story Mrs. Spicer reeled off was such a crock of beans. I mean talk about corny, I thought the Major'd see right through us in a flash and pretty soon we'd be on a bus back home. But instead, he says, sort of sly like he knows it's all just so much bull but he likes the careful planning it takes anyway, he says, "Well, well, I see," and puts his hands behind his back. He's got a newspaper rolled up in one fist and he rocks back on his heels and taps his leg with it—this way you can tell he's thinking, like when he'd smoke his pipe and you'd know it'd be an interruption to say anything to him. "I see," he says again, and, "Understood," like he's really thought it through. "Mind you," he says, "I don't necessarily agree with you in principle, but if that's your choice, I have to admire your tactical skills. Did Mrs. Spicer say you found her—or, I'm sorry, *she* found *you*—at the laundromat in town? Have I got that right?" He's looking at Jacky, but then his eyes shift back to mine like he's giving me a signal. That's when I started giggling, I mean I couldn't help it, even though there was supposedly nothing at all to laugh about—so I started coughing instead. Major Spicer steps over beside my chair and starts patting me on the back, like congratulations or something, and that makes it even funnier. So to stop laughing, like I've got to clear my throat, I take a sip of milk—which of course is a big mistake. The next second I'm spitting a white stream across the table, holding onto the edge and wrinkling up the smooth oilcloth to keep from falling over. Jack's wiping milk off his face with a blue napkin, real cloth, and he's glaring at me, and the Major's stroking my back now, almost like some guy looking to see if you're wearing a bra, and saying, "That's all right, go ahead and laugh, little sister. It's a good release." That's what he called me the whole time, except maybe once—"little sister." Did he know me and Jacky weren't really lovers but brothers and sisters instead? Maybe not, but he sure gave you the feeling that whatever anybody else said, it was all just so much bull— you and him knew what the real score was. But keeping up appearances was part of the game, like one of the rules or something. I mean he never said anything rude and he never lost that stiff Army posture of his either, the way he'd bend over from the waist, his back just as straight as a doll's anytime he'd reach down to scratch one of the family dogs or cats that were all over the place, laying around with their heads on their paws or sitting there staring up at you like you're going to give them something good, maybe a crunchy dog biscuit or a pat on the rear. It was real homey the way the dogs rubbed up against you, panting and grinning like they were just tickled to death you were there. If you think the yellow light in that laundromat was cozy, this was something entirely else. After a while that house really gave you the feeling of living in a beehive—Mrs. Spicer was this bustling queen bee with all these other bees buzzing around making honey—and Major Spicer off to one side, maybe, like the beekeeper with the net helmet to keep the bees from stinging him and getting in his eyes. Nothing ever really seemed to faze Major Spicer—no matter what crazy stuff was going on, he was above it all, outside of it entirely. For instance, the next thing we knew there was a lot of barking outside and some little kid is screaming his head off, but the Major doesn't even move. "There, what did I tell you?" Mrs. Spicer says. "Bertha won't put up with that kind of nonsense, they should have known better." Major Spicer laughs and says, "If they don't, they're finding out now, aren't they? Experience, Rhea, that's the only way we ever learn anything in life—as our adventurous young couple here bear witness. Those boys will pay closer attention in the future. A good object lesson if you ask me." Mrs. Spicer might have been listening to all this but I doubt it—she was already on her way out the door. In another second we could see her through the window waving at little Wendell and William with a broomstick she must have picked up on the back porch. We couldn't see the kids from where we were, but we could sure hear them. The barking had stopped as soon as Mrs. Spicer yelled, "*No,* Bertha, *bad* dog," but the screams were just getting louder, and we could hear the other kid, who turned out to be Wendell, the four-year-old, saying things like, "I *told* him *not* to," and "We didn't even *touch* her, we just wanted to *play.*" Mrs. Spicer bangs the broomstick down on the porch and says, "Mind your own business, sir, and leave Bertha to mind hers," and in a different voice she says, "There, there, you're all right, William, Bertha's not going to bite you." Major Spicer is chuckling and he's still standing beside me with his hand on my shoulder. I could smell his particular odor, like the smell of a pillow, beneath the other odor of tobacco and Old Spice shaving lotion that I can recognize anywhere and that always makes me think of Daddy. His fingers were absent-mindedly stroking the back of my neck under my hair, the same way you might pet a dog. It didn't feel personal at all, just friendly and offhand, so I didn't mind it, I like to have the back of my neck stroked, who doesn't? But Jacky looks over and lifts his eyebrows, so when I see nobody's looking, I stick my tongue out at him. Jacky just smiles and shakes his head like as far as he's concerned I'm some kind of moron. That look of his always makes me mad, but in one way I guess it turned out he was right. And I have to admit I never expected anything like what happened—in fact, I get so embarrassed I feel like one big blush whenever I think about it. This is getting into the stuff I'm not sure how to put in my letter—if Jacky ever lets me write one. The thing is, I don't want to just break the news to you, I want to tell you exactly how everything actually happened so you'll see it wasn't really anybody's fault. I mean finding fault is just picturing things according to some story where one way is automatically right and the other way is automatically wrong, but what I'm saying is that these particular things just naturally happened the way they happened, that's all. It made me feel sort of confused, but, honestly, in another way I really didn't mind, I was following right along with it. That was the next afternoon, after we'd spent the night there and eaten four more meals: lunch and dinner the first day, and then another breakfast and another lunch the next. Mrs. Spicer came up with the solution of whether she should let me and Jacky sleep together—because of course we weren't married yet, even if I *was* supposed to be pregnant. What she did was put us in bunk beds out on the sleeping porch with about half-a-dozen visiting grandchildren. It would've felt like a summer camp except it was all one big family, and they treated Jacky and me just like honorary members of the tribe. Major Spicer even asked me to say grace over lunch the next day. We were sitting at a long oval-shaped table, Jacky and me and about umpteen grown-ups and kids, out on what they called the dining porch. In front of us were these big yellow bowls of chicken-corn soup—really more like a chicken and corn and dumpling stew (Mrs. Spicer said they always ate a lot of corn in the summer)—and besides that there was sour-cream cabbage slaw, and sliced tomatoes in vinegar and sugar, and fresh-baked rolls, and—set out in these special little scallop-edged serving dishes—home-canned apple butter and molasses. It was great. Everything about that place made you feel terrific, it really did.

What happened was that after lunch that day Mrs. Spicer took Jacky along to help her pick some peaches, and, well, Major Spicer and me didn't even hear them when they got back. There were always people going in and out anyway, and we were upstairs way over on the other side of the house in the Major's personal study. I liked Major Spicer, and it's true he reminded me a little bit of Daddy. But I don't think I could ever really confuse the two of them, at least not the way the Major mixed me up with the girl in the picture. He was showing me through this big album of photographs at the time. Lots of old black-and-white pictures, starting with ones of his family and then going on to what he called his overseas tours in the military—this one I particularly remember of him standing in a flat bright place with his hands behind his back and wearing one of those helmets like Ramar of the Jungle. That was in North Africa during the war, he told me. The album was a kind of personal scrapbook. There was a dim, brownish one near the beginning of his mother and father—her standing in an ankle-length dress near the spout of an old hand pump, an arm held up to shade her eyes as if what she was looking at was too bright for her to look at straight-on—him standing beside the pump handle in a three-piece suit, one foot forward and a hand stuck into the arm hole of his vest like he's about to make a speech on the Fourth of July. There was page after page of newspaper clippings about Major Spicer from the sports pages and large group-portrait shots where he was a member of some team or other. In a specially clear one he was sitting at the center of the first row of his hometown baseball team holding a bat. Everyone had on a striped shirt and knee-socks, and they were all arranged on the seats of a wooden bleacher. To the sides and behind them you could see the trunks of trees, the tiny little crooked lines in the bark focused so sharp the trees took your attention almost as much as the faces. When Jacky walked in, we'd been looking at a photograph of a girl sitting in a tree swing. She had on a long white dress and was sitting sort of sideways, leaning against the rope so one knee rose up against her skirt. Her arms were stretched kind of lazy-like across her lap, a branch of wild flowers in one hand, maybe blue chicory or ironweed or some kind of aster, the stalk dangling so a blossom almost touched the ground. Her hair caught the light and was held back from her face by a wide, dark ribbon. This was someone I reminded him of, that's what he was telling me, someone he knew when he was still in school, before he joined the Army, way back before the war. And she really did look like me, she could have been my old-fashioned double. Her name was Audrey Cavanagh, his first love, so ethereal, he said, like a little faun, and she was built like you, he said, a fine round bottom for such a narrow girl, and his hand moves from my waist where he's been occasionally touching me to help direct my attention to some particular photograph, him seated in the swivel chair, me standing there beside the desk, and he slides his hand down over my rear end just like that, like he's sculpting clay. And I still don't move, not even when after a while his hand strokes up the inside of my leg and I feel his finger and thumb slip up inside my shorts—I was wearing those loose khaki ones with the wide cuffs and the big pockets. I put one hand on his shoulder like I was trying to keep my balance, that's all I did. He was touching me so lightly I almost had to push against him to be sure he was there. Him talking all the time, and me still listening—as if the other thing with his hand is happening to somebody else. One minute he's talking to the girl in the photograph, saying things like, "Ah, Audrey, you're still as lovely as an angel, perched there in your swing," and the next minute it's as if he's talking to me, calling me by her name and at the same time feeling me up like it's open season on ducks or something. The way the desk was facing out a window meant we had our backs to the door, which also must have been unlatched, because neither one of us even heard it when Jacky came in. There's no telling how long he'd been standing there watching us, but long enough I guess. I bet we made a pretty picture from over by the doorway. It wasn't until the Major turned so he could nuzzle up against my chest that we saw Jack. He's just standing there pop-eyed in the doorway, like he's suddenly remembered something important he forgot to do. You almost expected him to snap his fingers. We were all frozen that way for a second, caught in this burst of something, not light but almost as bright and quick as when a flashbulb goes off. And then everything picks up again all of a sudden right where it left off, and there's voices and sounds again and everybody's moving in different directions. Me, I've got myself backed up against this big globe of the world on a wooden stand right there beside the desk. The globe was so big it came up to my waist, and I had my hands behind me holding onto it. I'm spinning it slowly, feeling the relief map of the mountain ranges slide by beneath my fingers, and I'm thinking, almost like a joke: even if part of me *is* in the United States of America, the other part of me is probably over in China somewhere, all the way over on the other side of the world.

What happened next was, one of the married daughters—everybody called her Sissy—I think her married name was Northman or Newman or something like that, she was little Wendell's mother but she'd left her husband just a couple weeks before, it was a big family scandal at the moment—anyway, Sissy comes waltzing in right behind Jacky and she must have bumped up against him or something because both of them jumped like they'd been hit by electricity. When Jacky jumped, it startled me so I pushed the globe right out of its socket and it bounces once and then rolls over across the floor toward where the Major'd come to a halt after he'd left his chair. All of us are looking at this big colored globe of the world, blue and green and brown and yellow, and the Major bends down and lifts it up off the floor with both hands to see if any damage has been done. "Is it okay?" I ask. I feel like I have to say *something,* so I say, "I didn't know it could slip out like that." "Just a slight dent, hardly noticeable," says the Major. "Right smack in the middle of Greenland. Nothing there anyway." Jacky looks up at him and smiles, just as cool, as if butter wouldn't melt in his mouth. "You can probably get it to pop out again if you just apply a little heat," he says. "Like holding a match to a ping-pong ball." Sissy laughs and says in a little-girl voice, "Will Daddy kiss the world and make it all better?" And the rest of us laughed too. Ha, ha, ha. Everything seemed like it was just hanging there again for a second, and then Sissy says, "It's so hot, I sent Buddy up to bring down one of your picture puzzles, preferably a snowy Currier and Ives. We're going to take it out on the east porch and try to cool off a little. Then I remembered Mama put all those old puzzles up in the attic. Sorry to barge in and startle everybody. My, it's warm in here, isn't it? Daddy, you ought to turn on the window fan if you're going to spend any time up here. Peggy Sue?" she says to me, "you look like you could use something with ice in it." So Jacky went first and then Sissy followed me and him out the door, and we left the Major still standing there holding his globe in his arms. The way he was holding it made the world look like a big Buddha's belly. The little dent where Greenland was could've been its navel.

So Jacky and me never really had a chance to talk right then. Sissy sent him up to the attic for a jigsaw puzzle and then she says to me, "How would you like some good old country lemonade?" and grabs my hand, and the next thing I know the three of us are out on the porch on the shady side of the house sipping ice-cold lemonade through straws. There's a big cut-glass pitcher all fogged-up and sweaty sitting beside us, and we're scattering out the cardboard pieces of the puzzle on a folding table, each piece glazed and colored on one side and dull pink on the other. We're trying to separate all the edge pieces first, looking for straight lines against all the knobs and sockets of the regular pieces. Because of how we're sitting, I'm working on a side edge, Sissy's working on the snow-covered bottom part, and Jacky's got all the blue pieces of sky. The picture's called "An American Homestead Winter," and there's lots of white, but there's other colors too: a few reds and lots of greens and browns and yellows, and about a million different tones of grayish-blue shadow. The picture on the cover of the box shows these sort of waxy-looking people going about their chores, gathering wood, carrying a bucket, feeding cows and ducks in the snow. A brown dog that looks a lot like old Bertha, but younger, is prancing along beside the man carrying the kindling, and to his right there's a red horse-drawn sleigh with a man in a blue coat holding the reins, and next to him a lady, probably his wife, with some kind of a pink bonnet tied under her chin. They're passing a farmhouse set on a low hill by the road. It reminded me of the Spicers' house a little bit. I was thinking it looked like their house might look after a snowfall. I'm concentrating as hard as I can on the puzzle so I won't have to think about the other stuff. I'm looking for pieces of twisty brown forest with a straight edge on one side. I don't even glance over at Jacky because I'm not ready to meet his eyes yet, I'm not sure how he expects me to act. But what the heck, nothing much really happened. And why should *I* be embarrassed? I didn't do anything. That's what I think, but there's no telling what Jacky thinks, which is what always throws me off. But we're all working on the puzzle so we don't really get a chance to look at each other much anyway. Instead, we're looking back and forth from the picture on the box to the skinny sections of connected puzzle pieces in front of us. It's like we're working on three different puzzles instead of one big one. OVER FIVE HUNDRED PIECES, it says on the box, SCROLL-CUT AND INTERLOCKING. "So I see Daddy's been showing you his trophies," Sissy says to me. "That's a sure sign of favor—if you can sit through it. There!" she says, pushing a piece of shadowy snow into one of her little sections. "A corner! Now we're starting to get somewhere. All we need is the corner on your side, Peggy Sue, and we'll have almost half the frame! Buddy, I hate to say anything, but your sky appears to be upside down." "Hah!" Jacky snorts. "From where I'm sitting it's everything else that's upside down." Sissy laughs like she's been taken by surprise. "You're absolutely right," she says, "Everything *is* relative." She's got on glasses with turquoise frames, and she points a finger between her eyebrows to push them back up her nose. Her hair's so brown it's almost black and it's cut short and curly. She reminds me a little of Audrey Hepburn—real thin-boned and aristocratic-looking. She must be distracted about something though because she lights a new cigarette before the last one's finished burning. When she exhales, her nostrils flare out, and then she reaches up and picks a fleck of tobacco off her tongue. "Well, it's almost Wedding Day Eve! You love birds must feel like you've got the world on a string, sittin' on a rainbow—isn't that the way the song goes?" She moves a piece of puzzle around and when she can't find a fit tosses it back onto her little pile. "I bet you can't wait to get into Maryland and tie the knot that binds, right? Make it official in the eyes of God, man, and the PTA." Jacky just laughs and says, "It'll probably take a couple of days once we get to Maryland to get a license and everything." "Well," she says, "I wish you all the luck. At your stage, it's all bill-and-coo and rub-a-dub-dub. Believe me, I know all about it, and I say enjoy it while it lasts. Seize the day. Just don't take all that hot britches stuff too seriously. I'm not saying this to shock you, but—look, take my advice and go to a good drugstore instead of a justice of the peace. Go ahead and have all the fun you want—just don't get married unless you absolutely have to." She's found a piece that fits and she taps it in with a clear-polished fingernail. Her nails aren't long but they're so perfect they make me curl my fingers. My own nails are pretty raggedy-looking, even though I've been trying to only chew them when they need trimming. Her fingers have yellow tobacco stains though. She'll forget she's holding a cigarette and it'll burn right down to the skin. "What makes you think we've got such 'hot britches?' " Jacky asks. He's got his elbow on his knee and his chin in his hand and he's looking up at Sissy like she's the light at the end of the tunnel. "I mean, why do you think that?" Over across the yard we can hear some kids playing guns in the woods. "Pa'*dow!* Pa'*dow!*" one of them yells. "I *got*cha!" "You did *not!*" "I did *so!*" Sissy gives her surprised laugh and raises her glasses to the top of her head so she can look at Jacky eye to eye. "Because, as my mother always says—and what higher authority can there be?—'when peaches get ripe they fall off the tree.' " She raises her eyebrows and nods her head in a quick gesture she uses a lot—it's like her mother's "Amen." "I'm not saying you're wrong," Jacky smiles. "In fact, I'd have to say you're probably right, but is that just a generalization or are you talking about me and Peggy Sue in particular?" "Well, if the shoe fits . . . ," Sissy smiles back, ". . . it might as well be yours—no?" She lowers her glasses again and looks down at the puzzle. "Peggy Sue, what do you think?" she asks. "Does the shoe fit?" "I guess it both does and doesn't," I say. I'm a regular little diplomat. "I'm not exactly sure what shoe you're talking about," I say, "but it probably doesn't fit as good as this," and I push another piece into a string of about ten or twelve that was my main section of edge, twice as long as any of theirs. Sissy falls back into her rocking chair and takes a drag on her cigarette. "Don't be too sure," she says. She rests her elbow on the arm of her chair and touches the tip of her cigarette to the tip of her thumb, and as she breathes out smoke she just openly sizes Jacky up—the way somebody might look at something they wanted to draw. "I just meant that you're, you know, young and healthy and in love, and there's bound to be a certain, let's say . . . physical attraction, *n'est-ce pas?*" Jacky doesn't say anything for a second. They're both just staring at each other. I mean I almost felt like a third wheel. "Is that how it was with you and your husband?" Jacky finally says. "But of course!" laughs Sissy. "That part was sheer bliss. At least it was at first. But as it turned out, we really didn't have much else in common. When the other wore out, there wasn't a hell of a whole lot left." "The other?" Jacky asks. I can sense Sissy smiling at him more than I can actually see her. "Hot britches," she says: "Rub-a-dub-dub." And she wags her cigarette back and forth with her thumb. "Uh-huh, uh-huh," Jacky says, nodding his head. I'm still working quietly away on my pile of edges when Sissy suddenly sits up straight and reaches for her lemonade. She rattles the ice, then purses her lips to the straw and sips the lemonade down until it sputters in the ice cubes like a little motor. She's got her eyes back on the puzzle now, and she says, "Look at Peggy Sue! She's found the other corner!" Then, after studying her own sections of white bottom pieces for a minute, she taps a piece with the pink nail of her middle finger and says, "If this fits that, I think we can join sides." She places it real gently and pushes it in. "Yes! Perfect fit! How's that? Now we've got the bottom and one side—all we need is Buddy's blue sky and we're halfway home!"

I don't know where the Major was. Maybe he was still in his study, staring at Greenland. The three of us sat there working on the puzzle all afternoon and at one time or another almost everybody else in the family stopped by to put in a couple of pieces, but we never saw hide nor hair of the Major. We worked on the puzzle until it was almost suppertime. There were lightning bugs under the trees across the lawn by then, and it was getting hard to see. We could have turned on a lamp I guess, but nobody thought to. All we had left to fill in was some of the snow and a section of the sky. Except for that, the picture was almost done. It could have been either a sundown or a daybreak scene because there was a lot of pink in the sky, along with the blue. I tried to figure out which it was, morning or evening, but you couldn't really tell. It probably didn't matter. When I asked Sissy what she thought, she said, "Who knows? Maybe it's one of those long winter twilights that last all day. You know the kind I mean? Mmmmm . . . days like that always make me feel so romantic." She arches her back like one of the cats stretching and then suddenly widens her eyes and laughs. "Don't misunderstand," she says. "I only mean days like that make me want to curl up on a davenport somewhere next to a crackling fire with a pot of steaming tea and a good, long novel—something Victorian maybe—although, come to think of it, there's not a wisp of smoke coming from any of these chimneys . . . I wonder why." "Where there's no smoke, there's no fire," Jacky says, whatever that's supposed to mean, and we're all three sitting there in the dark giggling like idiots when Mrs. Spicer calls through the window screen: "Supper's near about ready, Sissy, if you fellows want to wash your hands." "Thanks, Mama," Sissy says, and then she looks across the table at Jacky and me, raises her glasses to the top of her head, and grins. "Oh, *screw,*" she says in a way that sounds really sexy. "It looks like we won't get to finish what we started. And we came so close too." Nobody says anything for a second. Jacky leans back from the table, and right at that instant the crickets started up, like a ringing in your ears. It was a real warm evening. The stars were coming out and the sky was a thick, deep purple. There wasn't a breeze to be had, and the skin under my leg kept sticking to the cane seat of my chair. Through the window we can hear people moving around inside, chairs scraping against the floor, a drawer opening and then the sound of silverware. "Mom?" somebody's calling. "Where *are* you? Ma-a-*um!*" Sissy sighs and says, "Well, it was nice while it lasted, wasn't it?" Then she calls inside, "Here, lover, mother's out here, just a sec." She turns back to us and says, "He probably fell in the creek. He's always getting his feet wet. From wet diapers to wet sneakers," and she laughs. "You'll find out, Peggy Sue. You'll be me before you know it." Right then, click, a lamp goes on inside the window and some of the light spills out onto the card table. Except for where the table shows black through the unfilled holes, the light makes the glazed surface of the picture puzzle shine so that the snow looks almost real.

When we went in to supper, there was the Major sitting at the head of the table just as if nothing had ever happened at all. He's smiling that same crinkly smile and sniffing at the ham roast like he's posing for the cover of the *Saturday Evening Post.* Real wholesome and homey. When he said grace, he ended the prayer with: "And thank You too, Lord, for the sweet gift of love that is so deeply impressed, by Thy will, in the bosom of each and every one of Thy children . . . In Christ's name, Amen." I mean you had to hand it to the guy. And Jacky and me are playing right along—except Jacky's voice gets this little edge sometimes. He'll say stuff that means one thing to him and me and Sissy, another thing to him and me and the Major, and something else entirely to everybody else. Like when we had fresh sliced peaches with sugar and cream for dessert, and Jacky says, "Peaches may fall off the tree when they're ripe enough, but we picked these, didn't we, Mrs. Spicer? Sissy, how do yours taste? How about yours, Major? Ripe enough?" I think Jacky might have made him nervous, because right after supper the Major offered to take everybody into town to see *Ben-Hur,* which they'd all been dying to see for weeks, I guess. Me and Jacky'd already seen it twice, so when it looks like Sissy's going to have to stay home with little Wendell, Jacky volunteers us to babysit.

"We'd just like to repay some of the hospitality we've been shown," he says. "Goodness, what a young gentleman!" says Mrs. Spicer. So Sissy got to go to the movies with the rest, and we ended up having to put Wendell and his little friend William to bed. William had gotten permission to stay over and keep Wendell company. Anyway, it wasn't until they finally fell asleep after a last drink of water and a Peter Pan storybook and a pillow fight that Jacky and me had a chance to be alone. And I could see right away he didn't want to talk about me and the Major at all. Instead, he looks up and says, "Want to see something neat?" We're sitting at the kitchen table eating a second helping of peaches and cream, which we'd brought out of the refrigerator as soon as we knew the coast was clear. "Sure . . . like what?" I say. "Like follow me, I'll show you," Jacky says. We drop our plates into the soapy water in the sink, and Jacky grabs a long red flashlight from a shelf near the back door. I figure we're going outside and I start to turn the knob, but Jacky shakes his head and says, "This way, little sister, this way." I didn't like him calling me that, but I followed him anyway. We went out the kitchen to the hallway and then up the front stairs to the second floor. We're tiptoeing past the door to the sleeping porch where the kids are and Jacky's got the flashlight in one hand and he puts a finger to his lips with the other, and I suddenly felt like we were robbers. I got a sort of butterflies feeling like I had to go to the bathroom. We're passing another door when Jacky stops, turns, and pushes it open. It's a lady's bedroom, you could tell just by the way it smelled. "I think Sissy sleeps in here. Want to look around?" he says. "Is this what you wanted to show me?" I asked. "What's so neat about this?" "Shhh!" he whispers. "Keep your pants on." Then instead of turning on a lamp, he switches on the flashlight and shines it around the room. The beam of light was almost like something solid, like a stick that Jack could poke around with. He pokes it over some stuff on the night table—a crocheted doily, an empty glass, a Kleenex box with a white tissue puffed out part way through the opening—pokes it on over to the bunched-up pillows against the headboard, then on down the bed itself—which has a purply patchwork comforter that looks like somebody's been laying on it—on down across the floor to a little pile of clothes near the dresser. On top are the navy blue shorts Sissy was wearing earlier—inside-out now with the pocket linings showing—and a pair of pearl-colored panties. "What are we doing?" I asked. "Just looking," Jacky says. "Well, I'm getting out of here," I told him. Sissy'd been nice to us and I didn't like nosing around in her room that way. So I turned around and walked out, and after another second here comes Jacky too. "Okay, let's go," he says, switching off the flashlight and pulling the door closed to where it was.

I have no idea what's on his mind at this point. I'm just hoping he doesn't want to steal anything. Our money was getting low and I was wondering how we planned to get some more—which I still am wondering in fact. But Jacky walks on down the hall and doesn't stop at any more bedrooms. Instead he takes me around a turn at the end of the hallway and we immediately come to a dead end at this closed door. The turn in the hall is really just a little nook with the door tucked in it. Jacky turns the knob and sweeps out his arm in this sort of cramped imitation of Reginald Van Gleason the Third ushering me into some fabulous mansion. All I can see is a staircase going up. It's like a tunnel, no wider than the door, and it's real steep. The stairs are made out of unfinished boards, so rough they look almost fuzzy, and they march up one after another into the dark. When Jacky points the flashlight, I can see ceiling rafters through the opening at the top of the stairway but that's all. While I'm poking my head through the door, Jacky leans over and—real quiet but right in my eardrum—says, "The *Sha*dow kno-o-ows," and then he does this spooky laugh. Eeyow, it gave me the creeps, and I didn't want to go nosing around in anybody's attic with a flashlight anyway—there'd probably be spiderwebs all over the place up there and who knew what all else, maybe even bats for all I knew. Even down there in the doorway I could smell the dust, and something else too, like the insides of certain old books, or like the woods. It was a smell that had layers to it, the way it might be if the smells of a whole lot of different rooms were piled all into one another. "Come on, Jill," Jacky says. He puts his hand on my arm and points the flashlight: "Look!" he says. "There's the signpost up ahead! Your next stop—The Twilight Zone!" He's got Rod Serling's voice down pat, and I'm laughing now, ready to go up and take a look. The spookiness isn't real anymore, it's like being inside a fun house now, and while we're climbing the stairs Jacky's doing his Mr. Magoo voice, saying stuff like, "Eh-eh-eh . . . yes, by Gad, the old homestead . . . I'd recognize it anywhere . . . chuckle-chuckle-chuckle," and I'm just laughing away, not even thinking about the stuff with the Major or anything else now. When we come up the stairs through the opening at the top, our eyes are at floor level, and from this angle especially the attic is pitch-black. We can only see where the flashlight makes a hole in the dark. There's a lot we can't see. Things just pop into sight wherever Jack happens to shine the flashlight. It's like he's showing his own movie with that light and also following along wherever it takes us. He's shining it around like he can lick up everything he sees with it or like he's pouring all this stuff out of the flashlight itself instead of finding what's already there.

From what I could tell, it was just an ordinary attic, but bigger and more crowded with junk—old bicycle wheels hanging from the rafters and all different kinds of chairs, stacks of *Life* magazines and *National Geographics,* wooden chests and mirrors and a huge bamboo birdcage in a metal hoop at the top of its own floor stand. "Can you believe this place?" Jacky says. "Isn't this incredible? When I was up here this afternoon I couldn't believe it. They must've been storing stuff up here since before the flood!" He's really revved up about it, and I can see what he means. I've never been in any place quite like it in my life, not really. It seemed like an ordinary attic at first just because it looked exactly the way I'd always pictured an attic *would* look, without ever really thinking about it or anything. Jacky moves his searchlight in a circle around the room and we can see the junk piled everywhere, with little aisles winding through it all, like paths in the woods, leading off to other sections of the attic we can't even begin to see from here. Piles of books and boxes, green steamer trunks with white stenciling and half a dozen tennis rackets, a pair of black rubber hip boots and a straw fishing creel hung up by a leather strap next to an old-fashioned baby buggy with a sun canopy and big, spoked wheels. Stuff even crowding into where the eaves of the roof come down close to the floor and make low little passageways and crawl spaces around the edges of the room. I bet we weren't up there more than a minute when we heard a sort of low stomach rumble of thunder. For a split second, the little half-moon windows in the gables of the attic all lit up like jack-o'-lanterns and almost at the same instant there's a giant crash of thunder that makes the whole attic sort of shake and creak and jingle. "Too much!" Jacky says. "What a great place for a ghost story!" He's whispering and probably doesn't even realize it. The windows light up again right then and there's another clap of thunder and then suddenly it's raining, the sound of it loud and steady, drumming on the roof right over our heads. We can hear it whishing against the sides of the house and gurgling down the drainpipes—a lot of little sounds that melt into one big one. Funny thing is, instead of making it spookier, the rain makes the attic seem all protected and snug, like someplace where it's always King's-X and bad things can't happen. "What if everything you ever had all ended up in one place?" Jacky says. "Like you could find anything you'd ever lost up here no matter where you lost it." "Yeah," I said, "that'd be neat. What'd you look for first?" "No, you don't get it," he says, "I mean you'd never even *need* to look for anything because it'd all be there already, like your whole life, all in one place, not spread out everywhere. That would be you—everything that was part of you all together." Jacky can go on like that all night, talking about some dumb theory or other, like the one about the galaxies expanding. Sometimes you think he's got to be kidding and it turns out he's dead serious. So Jacky's talking away and we're moving into some deeper part of the attic, almost like another room that the main one opens up into, when suddenly I see somebody standing there against the wall. It was like having the breath knocked out of you. I couldn't even scream, I just grabbed Jacky's arm and pointed, and when he shined the light over we saw it was only one of those sewing dummies in the shape of a woman. Whoever it was had a good figure too, maybe as nice as yours, Mom— and it was sort of like seeing them naked. That might sound weird but it's true. It could've been Mrs. Spicer before she got fat. Looking at it gave me almost the same feeling of spying I had in Sissy's bedroom. Jacky couldn't take his eyes off it. "Well, what have we here?" he says. He goes over and sets the flashlight down on top of a shelf so he's got his hands free, then he comes up to the dummy and cups his palms over the dummy's breasts. "Oh, baby," he moans. He puts his hands around its rear end and pulls the dummy up against him and starts humping

away like he's a dog going at your leg. Then he says to me, "What if
this was Sissy? Oh, man! Wouldn't that be something! . . . Just like
you and the Major." Finally, I thought, here it comes. I was beginning
to wonder if he'd seen anything or not. "Why'd you let him do it?"
Jacky says. "Did you like it?" I didn't know what to answer, so for a
second I just listened to the rain drumming on the roof. If this was
winter, I was thinking, the rain would be snow and in the morning
everything would look shiny and white, just like the picture on the
jigsaw puzzle. Jacky turns away from the dummy and I'm thinking he's
going to ask me again and I won't be able to avoid it forever, but
instead he says, "What if I did that to Sissy? Do you think she'd like
it?" I'm standing next to something soft, and when Jacky shines the
light over at me I see it's an old daybed with piles of woolen coats and
old uniforms and stuff on it. "I guess so," I tell him. "I think she
might have a crush on you." I figure if I can keep on his good side
about Sissy he won't want to talk about me. "Yeah?" he says. "Would
you let me if you were Sissy?" "Sure," I said. "What would it be
like?" he says—then, "Let's pretend you're Sissy and I'm me, like
when you taught me how to slow-dance. Show me," he says. And he
puts the flashlight down on some kind of old hope chest so the light
makes our shadows real long—they go all the way across the floor and
halfway up the opposite wall, like giants. Jacky comes up until he's
standing right next to me and he reaches up and touches his fingers to
my breast, real soft. I wasn't really, you know, excited or anything like
that, but my breast started to get all tingly, and I guess he could feel the
tip of it perk up, because he looks at me funny and says, "That's it,
isn't it? . . . does that feel good?" I sort of gulped and nodded and he
kept on doing it and then in a few minutes he started kissing me and
putting his tongue in my mouth, and I swear that's about the time I
knew I was lost. But then he stops all of a sudden and reaches in his
pocket. I thought he was only trying to straighten himself out down
there—I mean I could feel how stretched he was and how tight his jeans
must be, but instead he pulls something out of his pocket and holds it
over to the light. It's the pair of panties we saw in Sissy's bedroom. I
couldn't believe it. "Would you put these on?" he says. "Oh, man,
that'd really be something." I was getting excited too by then, and I bet
I never really do put this part in my letter, but I loved the way it felt to

get *Jacky* so excited. I mean when he saw me in those panties he starts moaning and groaning and then he's got his hands all over me and he pushes me down onto the pile of coats. I could feel a button on one of the uniforms poking up against my back. By now Jacky's pants are down and he's got my legs apart, and then, just like that, we're actually doing it. It hurt like anything at first, but pretty soon I got sort of numb and it was okay. The whole time, I could smell wool and I could hear these springs somewhere under us squeaking like little birds in a shrub tree. Compared to that, the sound of the rain seemed to come from real far off. It all happened so fast, but it seemed to take a long time too. I was thinking how much I loved Jacky and how good it felt to have him so close inside me, wanting me so much, when I hear him whispering in my ear, "Sissy," he's saying. "Oh, God, Sissy, you just love it . . . you just love it. . . ." *Sissy, Sissy,* he kept calling me, over and over again—until after a while I started to cry, I couldn't help it, and pretty soon the tears were coming like they might never stop.

The next morning we hugged everybody good-bye—everybody except the Major, that is, who never touched me again, not once after that one time—and we promised to write, and then Major Spicer and this old Army buddy of his drove us to Hagerstown and left us off at a Howard Johnson's motel. That was a couple of days ago and now we're in this falling-down old mansion I told you about—in Delaware or Maryland or maybe even Virginia. It's hard to tell exactly what state you're in around here, but we're right next to the ocean. The sound of the surf comes and goes just like somebody breathing. So now I keep thinking, maybe I really *am* pregnant. Can that happen between brothers and sisters, between twins? Or if it can, do you have to do it more than once? Because we only did it that one time, and since then we never even mention it and Jacky's gotten so he's real self-conscious about any kind of touching at all. It seems like we might as well be strangers—that's the worst part about the whole thing. I guess if I don't get my period that'll mean I'm probably pregnant. We'll just have to wait and see, right? If I *am* pregnant though, then maybe we can finally stop this wild-goose chase after Daddy and turn around. Sometimes I almost wish I *was* pregnant, because I'd really love to come home. Where we are now, there's always this fishy salt smell in the air. It'll go away but then it'll come back and you'll notice it again. Sometimes it smells great and other times it smells just like garbage. The ocean makes a steady whishing sound like rain against the rocks on the other side of the stone wall across the road. Jacky's out there somewhere trying to catch a bluefish. There's a lot of tall grass around here that looks like wheat. The feathery tips are a silver color, and I spend a lot of time just sitting here watching the way the wind ripples through them like they were made out of water.

Life Jackets

My mother and Mrs. Kincaid are trying to talk Doris into going with me to the evening movie, which tonight is outside on the top deck. The trouble is, it's a Western and Doris only likes musicals and comedies.

"I bet she'd go," I say, "if they had popcorn and M & M's like at home." I wish Doris would make up her mind because I'm in a hurry to get out on deck while there's still some daylight left.

"Honey, we're just going to be playing cards, you'll get bored if you come with us," my mother says to Doris. She's standing at the bureau mirror with her head tilted so she can put on her earrings and watch Doris and me at the same time. The earrings are gold loops with tiny gold hearts hanging off them. In the mirror my mother's face has a surprised look it doesn't have in real life. In real life, it looks more like she's getting ready to smile. "Don't you want to go to the show with Billy?" she says, trying to catch Doris's eye.

Secretly, I hope Doris *won't* come with me. Sometimes just having her around gets on my nerves. Which doesn't mean I don't like Doris, because I do—she's my sister. Once in a while I might wish Doris didn't exist, but then if I ever think even slightly about anything bad actually happening to her, I get so scared I can hardly breathe. Our first day on board the *Sultan,* we found out that last year, on the same trip we're making right now, the same time of year and everything, one day this kid just a couple years older than me let his little sister sit up on the rail of the promenade deck; then he turned away for half a second and when he turned back around she wasn't there. Just like that. One minute this guy's little sister is right there and the next minute, *presto:* she's gone.

"Would you rather come with us?" my mother asks.

Doris shakes her head but doesn't look up from where she's planted herself cross-legged on the floor next to her bed. She's picking at a callus on the side of her heel. Her toenails are painted a bright fire-engine red and she's bent down so close to her foot she looks like she might be getting ready to eat it. Which, really, is exactly what she *is* doing: every once in a while she'll pop a piece of skin right into her mouth. Doris you could say is on the chubby side, and you can usually count on her to be eating *some*thing. From where I'm standing looking down at her, I can see the blue, ribbon-shaped barrettes that hold her hair back from her forehead. A few years ago, her hair changed from nearly white-blonde to a sort of mousey-colored brown, and Doris couldn't have been happier. No more baby hair for me, she said. Now it's almost as dark as my mother's.

"Don't you like Kirk Douglas?" Mrs. Kincaid asks Doris. "I think he's a doll. I love to look at the little dimple in his chin." She says this as if Doris, who is only eight going on nine, ought to jump at the chance to go gaga over Kirk Douglas herself.

We first met Mrs. Kincaid because she was assigned to our table, and since then she's been hanging around with my mother night and day. They drink cocktails and play cards all afternoon and then, after dinner, they drink cocktails and play cards all over again while Doris and I go to whatever movie is showing. Even though she's younger than my mother, Mrs. Kincaid is married to a full colonel and she also wears a hearing aid. She's meeting her husband in Okinawa, just like we're meeting my father in Japan. She doesn't have any kids of her own, and she treats me and Doris like grown-ups some of the time and other times like babies. Her hair is long and real dark, with these red glints sliding around in it so she looks like she's moving even when she's sitting still. But what really gets me is this black wire that leads from the plastic thing in her ear to somewhere inside of her dress. I think sometimes she may be able to pick up extrasensory messages on it. Thought waves. A lot of times she'll get this funny smile on her face when she's looking at you, like she knows a secret about you nobody else knows. I've been trying to figure out some way of listening in on her hearing aid myself—then maybe I'd find out what sort of signals she's picking up.

She crosses her legs and takes a Viceroy cigarette from inside the purse on her lap. She's holding the cigarette out between the fingers of one hand and rummaging around in her purse with the other, probably looking for the lighter she can never find. It's a thin gold Zippo with a silver eagle on the front of it that means bird colonel. Mrs. Kincaid is always losing stuff. Yesterday, she lost the key to her stateroom and they had to give her a new one. All she said was, "It'll turn up, they always do." Now she snaps her purse shut, looks over at me, and winks. "How about giving a lady a light," she says.

"I'm not allowed to carry matches," I say, spreading out my hands to show her I don't have any. But then my mother takes a pack out of her purse and tosses it to me.

"There," she says. "I didn't say you weren't allowed, I just said I didn't want you playing with those bluetips."

On the matchbook cover there's a picture of a girl with a ponytail. DRAW ME, it says, and something about the picture makes you want to try. I light a match and hold it out to Mrs. Kincaid, but instead of lighting up, she puts her hand on my wrist and says, "Watch—I'll show you a trick." Then she puts the Viceroy up to her lips and leans forward so that if I want to I can see right down her blouse. The cigarette is still a couple of inches above the match, but when I try to raise the match up she presses my wrist and says, "Uh-uh." The cigarette isn't even close to the fire, but suddenly the tip bursts into flame and it's lit. The little brown flakes of tobacco are glowing bright orange.

"Presto," says Mrs. Kincaid, and she leans over and blows out the match with a stream of smoke that brushes my fingers like a feather. Then when she glances up she catches me looking at where the wire from her hearing aid goes into her blouse. She smiles at me that certain way again, and I can feel my face getting hot.

"That's pretty neat," I say. I start to turn away, but Mrs. Kincaid's still got her hand on my wrist. Instead of pressing, her fingers are just barely touching my skin—it almost tickles.

"Don't you want to know how it's done?" she asks.

"Sure," I say. She's trying to look me in the eye, but I won't let her. I keep looking back and forth from the burnt-out match in my hand to where the black lines in the floor tile go out like spokes all around my sneakers.

"It's because it's not the flame that lights the cigarette, it's the heat. Heat goes straight up."

"Straight up," I say. "And you can't even see it."

"That's because heat currents are invisible," Mrs. Kincaid says. She takes her hand away from my wrist and leans back in her chair.

I don't know what to say—I just want to get out of here. I flip the match into the wastebasket and put the matchbook in my pocket. "Come on, Doris," I say. "Maybe we'll see some whales if we get out there before it gets dark."

"Whales!" says Mrs. Kincaid. She stands up and the smell of her perfume swirls around us like a cloud. My mother has perfume on too, and the two different smells blend together until I can't tell which is which. "Wouldn't that be fun, Doris?" Mrs. Kincaid says. She swings around toward my mother. "I hope in my next life I come back as a dolphin—they always look like they're having such a ball. It makes you wonder what their secret is."

Mrs. Kincaid gets very talky after she's had a few drinks, but my mother usually gets real quiet and like she's waiting for something nice that's going to happen. Now she turns away from the mirror and looks over at Doris. "Honey," she says, "why don't you go with Billy? The movie won't be a scary one, I promise."

"But if she *does* come," I say, "she'll just have to stay till the end— we're not leaving the first time something scary happens—" When they showed *King Kong* Doris wanted to leave right after this scene where they're on a ship, just like us, going to the South Seas, and the blonde lady who's going to be in the movie they're making leans back against the deck railing so she's looking at something you can't see, and her eyes get wider and wider, and then she starts to scream, and she screams and screams and screams.

The bow lifts and we rock slightly toward one side, then it falls and we rock slightly toward the other. From up here on the top deck, we can see the horizon all the way around, one continuous circle, like a big flat plate we're right in the middle of. There's a strong breeze out here too, and the orange-striped cloth on one of the deck chairs is popping like a cap gun. Four sea gulls with long, black-tipped wings are riding the wind and squawking. They lift and glide, shifting around on currents you can't even see, their wings barely moving. The sun is already down but the sky still has a sort of reddish orange light smeared across it.

In front of us, the bow splits the water open, and behind us the split keeps spreading apart until it disappears. Up here it feels like you're on top of the whole world. The world is this circle we're in. Everything else—streets and cars and trees and all that—is gone. It doesn't exist anymore. If it *does* exist, what happened to it? It's nowhere to be seen. I'm not saying I actually believe this is true. I'm just saying it's a feeling I have right now, up here on the top deck. I can see eight sea gulls now, banking their wings and gliding through the air. I wonder how do their numbers keep changing way out here in the middle of the ocean? Where do they go to when you can't see them?

Doris and I are sitting over against the port rail. My left elbow points due south. There are about a dozen other kids up here besides us, but Doris and I stick to ourselves. Most of the boys already know each other from sharing rooms. That's because, on an Army ship, if you're over twelve you can't stay in the same stateroom with members of the opposite sex, even if it's your own mother. I still have a month to go, my birthday's in August. The guys who share rooms are always punching each other on the arm and laughing. Once, I heard them say my name in this real high voice—"*Bee-lee*"—and they all laughed. It sounded the way Doris says it sometimes, so maybe she's the one they were making fun of. That's what Doris thinks, anyway. All I can do is pretend not to hear them, but secretly I'm on their side; if I was one of them I'd probably laugh at us too. Tonight was lucky, though—we were already in our seats by the time they came up, and they hardly noticed we were here. Also, some of them are with their mothers, everyone sitting in rows, so they're quieter, sort of like being in church.

"Do you like that lady?" Doris whispers.

"Which one?"

"Mommy's friend," Doris says. "Mrs. Kincaid."

"I don't know, she's all right I guess. I just wish she *would* turn into a dolphin, and swim away somewhere."

Doris starts giggling, biting the tip of her thumb so she won't make too much noise.

"Shhh!" I tell her. "Look out there. Are those whales?"

We both look where I'm pointing, but it's impossible to tell.

"I thought I saw a school of whales out there. I thought I could see their waterspouts," I say. "And they had these smooth round backs, like giant sea turtles. I bet they could swallow you up in a single gulp."

"I don't see any whales," Doris says.

The stars are starting to come out, but there isn't any moon yet. The brightest thing is the ocean. It glitters and shines, always moving— sliding and twisting around like a bunch of black snakes swimming in mercury. For a second, the breeze dies down, and in the lull I can feel all the invisible currents of things fitting together like the little wheels inside a watch. A funny hush comes over us and then there's a loud hum and the white square lights up where the movie's going to be. Numbers are flashing on the screen, and all the kids start chanting them out, from eight down to zero. When it gets to zero, they all yell "Blast off!" just as the movie comes on. Which I'm glad to see is in Technicolor. So far they've all been in black and white.

Kirk Douglas is riding out of the distant plains while the credits come on and the theme music plays. Way behind him are the blue peaks of a mountain range, and he's riding toward us across a desert that's got cactus and boulders and sagebrush on it. On every side, all around the desert, I can see the ocean shining. My father likes Westerns even more than I do. His favorite actor is Rod Cameron— he says all it takes for Rod Cameron is one punch. I wonder how Kirk Douglas would stack up against Rod Cameron. What if it was Kirk Douglas against my father? Who would my mother pick? What if Kirk Douglas was secretly my real father, and my father was just this actor hired to stand in for him while my real father was acting in the movies? I don't know why they sent my father to Korea in the first place. He's not really a soldier even—I mean, he wears a uniform, but he works at a desk and makes out reports and things. He's in the Quartermaster Corps. He says the only time he ever shot a gun was on a rifle range. In World War II, before I was born, he was stationed over in the Persian desert, but he got a horrible case of boils on his legs that had to be operated on and he was sent home. They gave him a Purple Heart, the same as if he'd really gotten wounded. The actor my mother thinks my father looks like the most is Dick Powell. She always sounds slightly exasperated whenever she talks about my father, the same with our old Studebaker and the big green davenport that's too heavy for her to move. Sometimes I get on the davenport and rock back and forth until I'm wedged in the cushions so deep I feel like I'm going to suffocate in there.

The movie goes on for a while, and pretty soon Kirk Douglas is starting to like these two different ladies—one who works in a saloon and one who owns a ranch. The one who works in the saloon reminds me of Mrs. Kincaid. She wears these really low-cut dresses and spider-web stockings, and she drinks whiskey just like the men do. My mother hardly ever drinks very much at all, but with Mrs. Kincaid she does. What if Mrs. Kincaid gets my mother drunk, that's what worries me. Last night, when she came in from being with Mrs. Kincaid, we were in bed and Doris was already asleep. So she sat down on the edge of my bed and she was smiling and humming some song. "How's my boyfriend?" she said to me. She put her hand on my forehead and stroked my hair back and I could smell her perfume mixed in with the cigarette and alcohol smells and I got this funny feeling. For a second there I thought she was actually going to bend down and kiss me on the lips or something. It made me think of how Mrs. Kincaid looks at me sometimes. Since my father went to Korea, I'm supposed to be the man of the house, which is why I've been trying to think up some kind of charm against Mrs. Kincaid, to keep her from changing my mother into anything bad.

All of a sudden, I notice there's a commotion going on. Sailors are running up and down the stairs and people are turning around in their seats. Now the movie screen goes blank, and over the loudspeaker comes this loud whistle: "*Too-whee! Too-whee!*" Then this voice comes on. "*Fire . . . ,*" it says. "*There is a fire . . . all passengers report to lifeboat stations . . . this is not a drill . . . this is not a drill . . . there is a fire . . . fire. . . .*" The alarm horn starts honking and everybody's standing up pushing chairs around and trying to get into the aisle.

I'm not sure what to do. I feel like running but I'm not sure where to go. So far we've only had one lifeboat drill, and what we did then was put our life jackets on in our room and *then* go to our lifeboat station. That's what I mean—here we are with the ship on fire and my mother is nowhere in sight. To keep Doris from guessing how scared I am, I start humming the theme song from the movie. Everybody's talking at once, and I can feel Doris pulling on my arm. She's trying to tell me something, but I can't make out what she's saying.

I grab her hand and pull her with me in among the backs of the people in front of us. "Stay calm, stay calm," this one lady keeps saying over and over again. Another lady in front of us screams out, "Tommy! Where's Tommy?" and people start jamming up and pushing to get past her. This is when I notice that my humming has magic power. It's turning everything down to slow motion so Doris and I are gliding in between everyone else. They're all just lumbering along, but we magically whiz right by them. Behind us, the lady keeps screaming, "Tommy! Tommy!" but we're already on our way down the stairs to our own deck.

"Hold on to the railing," I tell Doris. "And start humming."

"What for?"

"Don't ask questions—just *do* it." That's something Kirk Douglas said in the movie, and as soon as I say it I feel lucky again.

When we get to our stateroom, I unlock the door and we go in, but there's nobody here.

"Let's get the life jackets," I say. "Mom'll probably meet us at the lifeboat station."

"Why'm I supposed to start humming for?" asks Doris.

"Just do it, all right, Doris? Is that too much to ask?" I'm humming and pulling the life jackets out of their compartment under my mother's bunk. They're bright orange with a lot of straps and buckles that are nearly impossible to figure out. "Just hang it around your neck," I tell her. "When you get to the lifeboat station, maybe Mom'll be there—if she's not, somebody else'll fix it for you—"

"Aren't you coming too?"

"I've got to go look for Mom, just in case. Maybe she's with Mrs. Kincaid. I'll take an extra life jacket and meet you in a couple of minutes at the lifeboat station, don't worry—"

"But why do we have to keep humming?"

"If you hit the right frequency, it makes everything slow down, okay?—but I think the frequency keeps changing—"

Doris rolls her eyes the way she always does when I tell her something she doesn't already know.

"I'm taking Miss Millicent," Doris says. She picks Miss Millicent up from her place on Doris's pillow and starts primping at Miss Millicent's hair, humming a little song to herself like she's at a tea party. She won't watch a scary movie, but now she isn't even scared.

"Look, Doris," I explain. "This is serious. We're not playing now, all right? You've got to go right to the lifeboat station—you know where that is, where we went before, Station C, right on this deck—and wait there, okay?—whether Mom's there or not—that way you'll be safe—"

She's pretending she doesn't hear me, but I know she's listening. Doris is always smarter than people think.

When we come out of the room, the alarm has stopped honking and the hallway is completely empty. Walking down it is like going down the aisle of a moving bus. Everybody else must be out on deck at their lifeboat stations already. We probably aren't even supposed to be *in* here.

"Okay, get going," I tell Doris. "I'll just be half a second."

I watch Doris's oversize rear end move down the hall. She's got a funny sort of pigeon-toed way of walking. "Hold on to the rail," I tell her for the billionth time, but she doesn't hear me—probably because she's humming to Miss Millicent.

I turn in the opposite direction. Mrs. Kincaid is on the next deck up, stateroom number 181. I can't believe how stupid this whole thing is. If it wasn't for Mrs. Kincaid, my mother would've been *with* us, the way she's *supposed* to be, and if my father was here this probably wouldn't be happening in the first place. I'm still humming without even thinking about it; I can't tell if it's working anymore or not, but I like the buzzing siren sound it makes in my ears. For one second, I see all this from some faraway place where it's already over with—but then I fall back into where I am now and I'm running.

When I get to room number 181 I knock on the door as hard as I can but I hardly seem to make a sound. Nobody comes, so I start pounding with my fists. "Mom?" I'm yelling. "Mrs. Kincaid? It's Billy. Are you

in there?'' Finally, I grab hold of the knob and start twisting, and when
I do I find out the door's not even locked—it swings open all by itself.

Inside, the overhead light is on and at first it looks exactly like our
room. I think I must have circled back by mistake. Except the air's
different in here. It feels heavy and wet, and there's the smell of oranges from a basket of fruit over on the bureau. They gave Mrs. Kincaid a basket of fruit because her husband's a colonel. I'm looking at a
bunch of bananas that have turned completely brown when I notice a
sound like somebody's singing or crying or something. I can hear it
now because I've stopped humming. And I can hear water splashing
too. It sounds like somebody's taking a bath, but I can't believe even
Mrs. Kincaid would take a bath *now,* with the ship on fire and everything. Then I see her hearing aid on one of the lower bunks. There are
clothes scattered on the bed too, including a white brassiere like the
ones my mother wears. The hearing aid is lying on the pillow. That
must be why she's in the bathtub, she never heard the alarm. She'll
really have to get moving now. And I'll be the one that rescued her—
maybe they'll even give me a medal!

This is what I'm thinking when out of the corner of my eye I notice
something moving in the porthole. Because it's dark outside, you can't
see through the porthole any better than if we were entirely underwater.
Instead of being a window, the glass works like a mirror now—and in it
I can see through the half-closed bathroom door to where Mrs. Kincaid
is taking her bath. She's lying back against the porcelain edge of the
tub with her eyes closed, and steam is rising off the water like smoke—
it's all around her head so I can't see her face very clearly. She's got
her hair all piled up on top of her head, and for a split second she looks
like the DRAW ME girl on the matchbook. I watch her hand rise up
dripping from the water and move to her breasts. Her other hand is
underwater, but I can see her arm going back and forth, the elbow
bending and unbending just above the surface of the water. Then all of a
sudden her back arches and her head strains forward so hard the ten-
dons stand out on the sides of her neck. And she just stays like that,
rocking and straining against something I can't even see. Her lips are
moving, but I still can't tell if she's singing or crying or what. So I
reach down, pick the hearing aid up off the pillow, and slip the pink
bulb into my ear. But what comes rushing into my head, clear as can

be, isn't her voice at all—it's the whispery voice of the ocean: "*Shhh,*" it says to me, "*shhh. . . .*" So I don't say a word. I don't move. I'm holding so still I don't even breathe. I just stand there watching the porthole mirror and listening to something that sounds like sobbing and something else that's like the sound the ocean makes when you hold the pink inside of a seashell up against your ear.

My mother is sitting with her legs crossed and leafing through a magazine. When I come up to her I'm out of breath from running so hard, but all she says is, "Hi, hon, how was the show?"

We're in the main lounge and everybody's just sitting around as usual—playing cards, talking, rattling dice over games of Parcheesi and Clue. I came racing in here at full tilt, figuring I'd cut through the lounge to get to our lifeboat station. When I finally catch my breath, I pant out, "Where's Doris?"

My mother looks up and turns a page in her magazine. She turns the page so slowly it seems to *roll* over. Whatever she does is always like that—like she's moving underwater. "I thought Doris went with you to the movie," she says.

"The movie? What about the fire? They said we were on fire—" I look around but the only sign of anything burning is the smoke from a Parliament cigarette in the shell ashtray next to my mother. I can see her lipstick marks on the recessed filter tip.

"It turned out to be in somebody's wastebasket," she says. "A lot of smoke, I guess, but not much damage—didn't you hear the all clear?"

"The all clear?"

"It came on just a minute or two after the alarm went off. Where've you been?"

"I was looking for you," I say. "I've got your life jacket right here—" Except I don't have it any more. When I reach for it, I'm reaching for the place on the bed where I laid it down when I picked the pink bulb up off the pillow. In my mind's eye I can see Mrs. Kincaid rocking in the bathwater while the steam rises up all around her.

"Billy?" my mother says. She closes the magazine over her thumb and leans forward. "Baby, look at me. Everything's okay. The life jacket'll turn up. The fire's out and everything's running along smooth as silk."

On the cover of the *Look* she's holding over her lap there's a picture of Doris Day. The same name as Doris and also her favorite movie star. What's scary is when you can feel things building up entirely on their own this way and there's not a thing you can do about it. Like you're floating down some lazy river, happy as a clam just to drift along with the current, and then, right when you think it's taking you exactly where you want to go, here comes the whispery roar of the falls. In *King Kong* there's this part where the guy making the movie and his leading lady are in the jungle escaping from King Kong by climbing down a vine that hangs over the edge of this cliff. They think they're getting away but really it's King Kong who's got hold of the other end and all the time they're climbing down he's pulling them back up.

"I've got to find Doris," I say. I take off my life jacket and roll it up as tight as I can, until it's like a thick orange club.

"She's probably back at the stateroom helping Miss Millicent eat the piece of cheesecake she saved her." My mother smiles and dips her head trying to catch my eye—one of the gold hearts makes a tiny flash next to her ear. "And if you keep that frown on your face, you'll get creases in your forehead like an old man," she says. When she laughs it's a chuckling sound, like water going over smooth rocks.

I give her back the smile she's looking for, but I think my eyes must slide away too soon because she immediately says, "Billy, is anything else the matter?"

"I just want to see about Doris. She might not know the fire's out yet either—"

"I know what," my mother says, and I can tell she's decided to humor me along. "You go to the lifeboat station and I'll check the stateroom. Doris is bound to be one place or the other." She puts the magazine on the table beside her chair and stubs out her cigarette against the pearly inside of the seashell.

"The thing is, if I hadn't had to go looking for you in the first place, if it wasn't for that—" I start to say. "And what about bridge? I thought you and Mrs. Kincaid were going to be playing bridge—" I'm afraid I'll start crying if I say any more. I can already taste tears in the back of my throat and my eyes are burning. If the ship wasn't on fire, I'm thinking, then maybe it doesn't count that I didn't tell Mrs. Kincaid— but what if it *does* count, then what? What if it does?

"Billy, listen, I know you've had a bad scare, and I understand how upset you are," my mother says. Her voice is very quiet and reasonable, very reassuring. "But nothing happened," she says. "Everything's all right. Nobody has to blame anybody for anything. Our bridge partners didn't show up and Connie went off to wash her hair, that's all."

I've got my hand in my pocket and I'm sliding the matchbook with the DRAW ME girl back and forth between my fingers.

"Here, give me that," my mother says. "I'll put it back where it belongs."

At first I think she means the matchbook, but then I notice she's pointing at the life jacket under my arm. On the table beside her, the stubbed-out Parliament is still sending up a thin, wavery column of white smoke. My mother smiles again to show me she's not mad, she understands. She's being very patient, even I can see that. She's standing there with little gold hearts dangling from her ears and her arm out, smiling, waiting for me to hand over the life jacket.

The Compass of the Heart

Peggy Landis was my father's girl friend in those days, but I was the one she called her "beau." My brother Toby was "Mr. Tobias." Peggy came from Georgia, and these old-fashioned or formalized pet names were one of the ways she had found to exaggerate her Southernness and thereby perhaps more clearly characterize herself. Ill at ease in any world but the one pictured in the Gothic romances she devoured, she had apparently discovered that irony (so blissfully absent from the books she read) might allow her to have her cake and eat it too. She could present the self she believed she was and at the same time, through caricature, she could disavow it.

She'd open the door to the basement and we'd hear the methodical shhh-shhh of a saw or the whisper of a wood plane. "Loren, sweetie?" she'd call down the rubber-treaded stairs. "My beau has graciously consented to take me and Mr. Tobias out for ice cream. Want us to bring you back some?" There'd be a pause while my father ran his thumb along a planed bevel or brushed the sawdust from the grain of a cut board. Then he'd call up: "How 'bout some of that butterscotch-ripple, and maybe a pint of fresh peach? Tell James my wallet's on the table by bed."

Once when I was getting some money from his billfold I found a rubber. It was in a foil packet with a picture of a Greek helmet on the front, but I knew what it was. I reached inside my pants and touched myself and then let Peggy Landis hold my hand when we walked to Higgit's for hot-fudge sundaes and a carton of milk. She said I was more of a gentleman every day and she bet anyone would think we were sweethearts out on a date.

My mother died when I was four. She died in childbirth, as the saying goes. She never came back from the hospital. It was my father who carried the baby home. He'd be talking on the telephone, molding the ash of his cigarette against the edge of an ashtray, and I'd hear him say into the receiver: "Yes, she died in childbirth." It was something I learned to repeat whenever strangers would ask the question. They'd shake their heads and say, "Oh, I'm sorry . . . ," but I kept forgetting what there was to be sorry about. My sorrow was drifting into a distance that widened each time the words were spoken, as if my mother's death were a place the words were moving us farther and farther away from.

Peggy Landis had come to Washington, D.C., from Augusta to work as a legal secretary, and she had brought her mother with her. Her parents had been divorced years before; Mr. Landis lived somewhere in the central part of Florida now. I had come to understand that Mrs. Landis was an alcoholic, though the only time I ever saw her she was wearing a long white dress and sitting in a garden in a fancy, wrought-iron chair, her gray hair tied in a neat, old-fashioned chignon. She appeared kind and wise, and I remember she seemed to recognize me. She said, "James, there you are," as if I'd been with her just a little while before and she was wondering where I'd gotten to. Then she patted the chair beside her and said, "Sit here. Where you can smell the lilies of the valley. I know you love lilies of the valley." It was getting on toward dusk, and in her white dress she seemed to glow, becoming more and more luminous as the twilight faded around us. I never saw her again, and I learned that such periods of sobriety were so rare as to be virtually nonexistent. It was difficult for me to connect the mother Peggy Landis complained about so bitterly with the gentle woman I'd seen in the garden, but they were apparently one and the same.

On the other hand, I got the impression that her father—or "Daddy," as she still called him, like a little girl—could do no wrong. She was always bringing us citrus fruit or gift cartons of smoked sausage and cheese he'd sent. The doctors had told her that he must quit smoking, and she was concerned about his health. She used to love sending him imported cigars from a tobacconist's specialty shop in Georgetown, but then she had to stop. She worried about what to send him instead, until my father suggested a coffee grinder and fresh coffee beans. Then she started sending fragrant little burlap sacks of exotic South American blends and chicory. There's no telling why her parents had gotten divorced, and during a time when divorces were presumably rarer than they are now, but I learned her father was what they called a "ladies' man." I remember that when I heard my father use that expression for the first time I didn't know what he meant.

I thought I knew quite a bit about Peggy Landis, though. I certainly knew as much about her family as I did about my own mother's and father's. My maternal grandmother died before I was born, and my father's parents lived in California. As far as I can recall, we only went to visit them once, a short time after Toby was born. My single memory is of a lemon tree that grew up right against their bathroom window. Sitting on the toilet, I'd look out at clusters of yellow fruit that were much larger than any lemons I'd ever seen. In my mind, my grandparents' house became only a storybook with pastel pictures of sugarplum trees. When I think the word "grandmother," I'm still less likely to call up an image of my father's mother than of old Mrs. Landis sitting in that garden at dusk, dressed all in white, her hands folded on her lap like a fine linen napkin.

In those days I liked to take whatever book I was reading into my father's bedroom—the room farthest from the staccato of the TV—and read lying on my side, one ear pressed into the pillow, an arm flung over my other ear like a swimmer doing the Australian crawl. Every time I turned a page, I'd have to turn over and reverse my position. Cut off from everything outside the focused circle of my attention, my mind would close down like the iris of a camera, before spiraling open into that special place behind the words.

So that night, when my father comes into the room, I have to unlock my arm from my head to come up from my book; it's like rising toward a surface that breaks abruptly into some thinner element in which words seem almost random and without weight, and where I feel impa-

tient with the assertion of each ordinary thing. Only objects have gravity here, everything else floats away.

My father stands next to the bureau that used to be my mother's. His
fingers smooth the varnished surface that no longer holds her clutter of
tiny, corrugated perfume bottles, tortoiseshell combs, her shiny tangle
of costume jewelry. Now there is only the oval tray of a mirror, as
vacant as an undiscovered lake. His hand lifts, carrying a cigarette up
to his pursed lips. He wants to tell me something. In the familiar gesture that is his prelude to speech, he inhales, and as he talks the blue
smoke drifts and unravels.

"What do you say we go to the mountains this weekend," he says.
The fingers that hold his cigarette run back and forth along the glossy
edge of my mother's bureau. The smoke zigzags above his hand.

"Great," I say. I'm sitting up now, holding a finger in my book to
mark my place. The book is called *Bob, Son of Battle.* It's about a
border collie in the highlands of Scotland who gets accused of killing
the sheep he's supposed to look after, and it's turned out to be a little
hard going for a book I consider beneath me.

"Well, Peggy's got ants in the pants again—spring fever, I guess. She
says the weather's been fine the last two weekends, and you know how
crowded it gets after Memorial Day. I think she just needs a couple
days, you know, a little rest from the old lady. It's been a pretty long
winter for both of them. Anyway, I figured, well, I'd better see how
you feel before I say anything to Toby, he'll start packing his knapsack
the first word he hears, you know Toby—"

The rhythm of his speech is a rush, then a stop, then another rush. In
between phrases he draws on the cigarette so that smoke leaks out with
the spill of his words. My father's voice always strikes me as somehow
awkward and unpolished. I have felt embarrassed by the sound of it
sometimes in public. I want people to know the solid, sure presence of
him when he's down in the basement on a Saturday morning measuring
the raw boards before sawing and nailing them into the shape of a table
or a chest of drawers.

"That sounds great," I say.

"Well, then, I'll tell Peggy it's definitely on for this weekend. I know
she'll be just as tickled as anything. I just wanted to make sure, you
know, check it out with you first—"

"Hey, Dad, it's starting again!" Toby is calling from the living room where they've been watching "The Waltons." Because John-Boy wants to be a writer, they can't understand why I don't love the show. They're sure I would if I gave it half a chance, so Toby tells me all the plots, always leaving things out and having to back up and fill in: "No, wait— I forgot—*before* John-Boy writes the school thing, he finds the note from this girl, Mary Ellen's girlfriend or something. Even though Grandma says she's just spoilt rotten, John-Boy's always sticking up for her—" I've watched it a few times, but I resent its power to make my own life feel fragmentary and unlucky.

"*Day-yud!*"

"Okay, okay—hold your pants on, pardner, here I come—" My father stands for a moment in the open doorway. The hall light is behind him so I can't see his face very clearly. "The Waltons" theme music suddenly swells to a blare in the living room. Toby has turned it up to prove his point: "It's starting, I *warned* ya—"

I can tell he's waiting for me to say something more. "She's right, there won't be anyone else up there this early. You can tell her I think it's a really great idea," I say. "And, Dad, would you please make sure the door's latched when you leave?"

"Sure thing."

He turns back to the familiar voices of the Walton family in the living room, pulling the door closed and clicking it shut. I don't move back to my book until I hear the volume drop to a muffled murmur on the other side.

Driving up the interstate northwest from suburban Maryland toward southern Pennsylvania, you come over a rise and the horizon suddenly dips and pulls away. You look across a valley of cultivated fields and orchards and scattered houses that cluster around the white steeples of churches like the toy villages people set up inside the circles of electric-train tracks beneath Christmas trees. Unless you are told, you might not realize that the banks of blue cloud settled low on the horizon are actually the mountains you are going to. Somewhere in that far mist you will make your camp while the wind makes a sound like a rushing stream in the pine branches high above you.

We might have disagreed about everything else, but Toby and I both loved the mountains. I think what Toby liked best, though, was something that appealed to me only vaguely and in the abstract: it was the reassuring feeling of self-sufficiency that camping gave, the way it lent significance to the simplest, most mundane and merely practical matters of everyday life. Toby liked to gather firewood, for example, or to fill the water sack with spring water and hang it swollen and dripping from a nail he himself had driven into a tree. He liked to hold the tent ropes taut while the notched pegs were hammered into the ground, and he liked fiddling with the kerosene lantern and peeling twigs to roast hot dogs or marshmallows over a fire he had learned how to build so that air could circulate from the bottom up. Toby was happiest when his body was in motion toward some specific goal. At the age of eight, a good four years younger than I was, he already took on more responsibilities and was certainly more reliable and levelheaded. While the others were setting up camp, I'd be likely to wander off into the woods, imagining naked Indians stalking deer through trees I could actually reach out and touch, and then, where voices gave way to bird song and insect buzz, imagining the erotic opportunities the woods might yield to lovers. The summer before, I had spied on Peggy Landis and my father when we were berry picking in a thorny patch of brambles and underbrush down by the lake. They were far enough away so that I couldn't hear what they might be saying, but, seen through a tiny gap in the screen of blackberry vines, their images were sharpened the way things are when you look through a pinhole in a piece of paper. Behind me I could hear Toby warning me to keep on the lookout for blacksnakes. "I bet they're all over the place in here, James. And poison ivy, too."

Up until the following May, the only addition to my sexual knowledge came from fiction. I had been masturbating for less than a year. In fact, it was the sight of Peggy Landis's hand—as perfect as fantasy, self-consciously stylized with long, flame-red nails and a languid way of holding her forearm and wrist that accentuated the elegant length of her fingers—it was the sight of that cupped hand stroking my father's fly, as I say, that originally put the idea into my head. In a flash I knew what my erections were for, I knew what they wanted. That cool summer night in the mountains I lay in my sleeping bag across from Toby and waited to hear the steady sighing that would mean he was asleep. Then I began stroking myself, my mind illuminated by the image of the way Peggy Landis's white hand kept time with the slow, uptilted back-and-forth grinding of her pelvis against my father's leg. My hips began to make the same motion and I knew I was right. I began to feel a burning sort of tickle at the soles of my feet that made me curl my toes, and then my whole body was curled and lit up with it. I was like a piece of crumpled paper that suddenly catches fire and then subsides into white ash with little darting veins of ember still flickering and going out after the rush of flame has vanished. This had happened in August, nine months before, and since then I had come across three or four discreetly erotic scenes in the historical novels I occasionally borrowed from Peggy Landis. She encouraged my reading, and I think she may also have liked the idea of guiding me in what she called matters of the heart. I remember especially vividly such a scene in a novel about the American Revolution. The young hero and a girl he barely knows are hiding out beneath some blankets in a sutler's covered wagon as it rocks along down a country road behind enemy lines. I'd had to look up the word "sutler" in a dictionary but I thought I knew exactly what was happening under the blankets, and the confirmation in print of what I still could hardly believe, in a book Peggy Landis had actually given me herself, was almost more than I could bear. It was as if I'd inhaled the fire this time. The heat filled up my chest in a rush so that for a moment I couldn't breathe. When I touched myself I was so swollen the pulse of it was exactly the same as the beating of my heart. I could almost imagine I was dying, but I was no more afraid of death than a saint who knows he's going to heaven.

"Every time we come up over this rise and see the whole valley spread out that way, I think I'm just going to faint." She might be draped on a Victorian divan trying to bring herself out of a swoon with an ivory fan, but in actuality Peggy Landis is slouched in a corner of the back seat of my father's Buick waving at her face with the ten fanned-out cards of a gin rummy hand. Her head is leaning against the window beside her so that she can only see the landscape askance, as if a more direct view might blind her.

I'm kneeling before her in the front seat beside my father, my elbows on the backrest catty-cornered from where she is. I turn from my own hand, which I've neatly arranged in two promising runs of hearts and clubs, a pair of jacks, the queen and ace of spades, and glance quickly over my shoulder. I'm nodding in agreement when I catch my father winking at me. For an instant I'm panicked, thinking: he knows—even though I've got myself pressed up against the seat so no one can possibly see: he knows. The blood is throbbing in my temples when he grins and says, "How 'bout it, James, if we got paid a dollar every time she fainted, why I believe we'd have to find ourselves another line of work, what do you say?"

I cover my momentary surge of panic by shoving the two spades in between my run of hearts and the jack of diamonds. I always like to alternate the red and black anyway. I want to answer my father's joke with a casual, offhand remark, but all I can come up with is: "Well, I guess there's a first time for everything." I'm not even sure why I've said this, and my voice is so rough I have to clear my throat. The blood has left my loins and gone directly to my face. I glance at Peggy Landis, but her dark glasses, curved up at the corners like a cat's ears, make it hard to read her expression. I can't tell if she's looking at me or not.

She nibbles at her lower lip for a second, the way she sometimes does when she's deciding whether or not to be offended. Occasionally, she'll get mad at the most unlikely things and lash out with something cutting, or sulk until she gets an apology. Her moods and reactions are so unpredictable they almost seem designed to bewilder us. One effect of this is that we can never take her feelings for granted; we have to keep checking back to make sure she's not angry or hurt or secretly laughing at us when we think we're being serious. Now she chuckles and looks over at Toby. He has his window down and the wind is riffling through his hair. It's cut so short I can see his pinkish scalp beneath the blond stubble. School's not even out yet, but he makes a summer ritual of cutting his hair as soon as the weather turns warm. That and getting a new pair of sneakers. The hieroglyphic soles of his black-and-white, ankle-high Keds (the kind my father says he used to wear) stick out from behind him as he sits back on his heels and turns from his open side window to the wide view of the valley through the front windshield.

"Boy, there they are. I can hardly wait." Toby stares straight ahead. He might be talking to himself as much as to any of us. He's actually licking his lips in anticipation.

"Now see there? Mr. Tobias knows what I'm talking about. These old stick-in-the-muds just think they've seen it all, but we know better, don't we, Toby?"

He may not have the slightest idea of what she means, but Toby always loves it when Peggy Landis makes him her sole ally. Now he pounds the backrest beside my elbow and laughs uproariously. "D'ja hear that, you old stick-in-the-mud?" he gasps. "That's you, James! Hah! That's you for sure!"

"Oh, shut up. What do you know?" This is my standard reply. I want to get back to the silent, breath-stopping game I've been playing with Peggy Landis for the past twenty minutes.

"Stick-in-the-mud. Old stick-in-the-mud James—" Snorting in what is now a somewhat forced glee, Toby turns back to the side window, raising up on his knees to stick his head out and catch the wind full face. He inhales deeply, as if he can already smell the pungent odor of pine sap and creek moss.

Looking back at my hand, I realize that I've got too many points and decide to get rid of the queen of spades. To keep them from sliding, we've stuck the discards faceup in the seat crevice next to Peggy Landis's right hip. I reach over and tuck the queen in on top of the pile. Peggy Landis is wearing white terry cloth shorts and I can see tiny, nearly invisible curls of hair like light pencil strokes on her bare thigh. She looks down at the new card, then back at her hand and shakes her head. "Nasty old lady. No thank you, Mama needs something a little lower than that. Give me the one I want, honey, give me just the right one."

When I reach down to where I've got the rest of the deck stuck in the crevice beside my knee, I am swollen again, I can feel the steady pulse of it where I'm pressed into the backrest. Trying to appear perfectly nonchalant, I peel off the top card and sail it directly at the soft V where Peggy Landis's thighs come together. This is what I wait for, it's almost as good as dealing, which is the best, when I get to toss one card after another at the same spot while her dark glasses stare back at me.

Now she takes the card from where it lies face down on her lap, smiles as she inserts it into the red fan she's holding with the long fingers of her other hand, slowly slides another card out, and then, in a gesture that abruptly rouses me from my trance, slaps it face down on her leg. "Gin," she says.

I sometimes wonder why, in my fantasy of a forbidden conspiracy between me and my father's girl friend, I had no particular sense of crossing a border into incest, however figuratively defined. After all, I knew that she was only a few years younger than my mother would have been, and mother was certainly one of the roles she liked to play. It's true also that whenever I was lusting after Peggy Landis, all I had to do was think of my real mother and I would flinch and almost writhe in shame. Nevertheless, my mother had become largely an abstraction, something for which I had language but only generalized and rehearsed emotion. My memory of her was a blank page I'd filled with words, and the only personal feeling the words generated was self-pity.

So, as far as I can remember, I felt almost no guilt on that score. On the other hand, I'm sure I wanted to get even with my father and Toby for the special closeness they seemed to have. Maybe something of what my father felt for my mother got into his feelings for Toby when she died giving him birth. Also, Toby had been sick with rheumatic fever. He still went to the doctor every few months for a heart check. In fact, Toby was really rather fragile. He wasn't an albino, but his complexion was so light I could always make him cry by calling him "The Pink Fink." My treatment of him would swing between extremes of torture and placation. I was always making up to him for something I'd done or, more often, for something I'd said. Or else I'd ignore him entirely and for days remain submerged in my daydreams and books. My father managed a chain grocery store in a shopping center not far from where we lived, and, as an example of the closeness between them, Toby kept up on all the new products—"gel" toothpaste and potato chips that came in a can, French-bread pizza and the different brands of "natural" cereal. The salesmen were always giving away free samples that Toby would test, and he knew all the commercials on TV by heart. He loved to walk up and down the aisles of the store checking prices and noticing the way everything was displayed. I hated even to go into the store. The fact that my father was everybody's boss somehow embarrassed me. I hated the attention the cashiers gave me, or, if they were busy, I hated being ignored. My father first met Peggy Landis when she asked to see the manager because she thought she'd been overcharged for three packages of lamb chops. She was right, as it turned out. She'd been charged for rib-cut rather than loin.

It still seems to me just possible, however unlikely, that Peggy Landis really wanted a passive twelve-year-old boy for her "beau." The thing is, I've always had trouble separating my fantasies about her from who she really was—especially since she always seemed to be playing a role anyway. In memory I find her caricatured, larger and more vivid than life, a character in a movie. But even if my attentions were invited, I must have felt like a traitor, betraying everybody I cared about most—my mother in some obscure way, my father clearly, and Toby if only because I wanted to fashion a triangle he'd be cut out of.

In any case, what happened that spring night in the mountains isn't hard for me to understand. It's what came after that, and the peculiar confusion that resulted from what I saw and heard, that I'm still trying to puzzle out. How can the heart's reckoning be so sure and yet so wrong? Or is it wrong if, by causing us to stumble and misstep, we are led finally to the truth? These are the central questions, it seems to me, and they lead me round and round. The simplest explanation, I suppose, must begin with the fact that it was a lot harder to hear on the second night because of the rain. The first night, on the other hand, was so clear I could see the mantle's incandescent filament burning in a white arc at the core of their turned-down Coleman lantern. It was so quiet I could even hear it hiss.

The two tents are set up on opposite sides of the campfire. Toby and I sleep in a pup tent with a triangular opening at either end. It's small and narrow, and our sleeping bags, lying side by side, fill up most of the space. Their tent is large enough to stand up in. It's hexagonal, with an entrance flap that can be extended in front like a canopy. The tents face each other but are offset and parallel rather than head-to-head. This way, each tent opens on woods instead of directly facing the other one, and there's also a little privacy.

Our faces are flushed and shadowy in the firelight. We're tired but excited after our recent exertion. It was nearly dark when we arrived and we had to set up camp in the waning twilight, the darkness much thicker here under the trees than out on the highway. Toward the end, we even had to turn on the car headlights in order to see what we were doing. Peggy Landis has brought a basket of her famous "Georgia-fried" chicken so we don't have to cook, but we've made a fire anyway. I gathered wood while the others unloaded the car and worked on the tents, and as soon as the tents were up we built the fire. It provides a necessary center, and now, in full darkness, its circle of light gives us an illusion of enclosure and shelter, pulling us back together now that we've finished our separate chores.

Always, on the first night, building the campfire would seem the very reason we had come. There is a picnic table at each campsite, but, partly because it's easier to see and partly because we're drawn as by a magnet, we are kneeling around the campfire like worshipers. Avidly, each in a private satisfaction beyond words, we are eating the delicious cold chicken. It's all white meat, just breasts and wings, each piece deep brown and crumbly with fried batter. I know the wings are especially for me. Peggy Landis has discovered how much I like them. This is one of our more open secrets, or so I imagine. Like an actress, she has a real talent for the devices of intimacy if not for intimacy itself: she knows that unspoken attentions are the best kind. When our eyes meet over the fire, we seem to be in such close communication that I have only to lick my lips in order to let her know exactly what I'm feeling. And she seems to feed on my satisfaction, as if that were really what she's savoring rather than the bite of chicken breast she's chewing.

My father wipes his hands on his jeans—something he'd never do at home—and clears his throat. But instead of speaking and breaking the fire-crackling silence, he lights a cigarette and stares moodily, sated and suddenly pensive, at the blazing sticks. One of them, apparently greener than the others, snaps fiercely and sends a spray of sparks out toward his feet. Meditatively, he extinguishes each of the embers under his shoe, but the offending stick keeps popping and fizzing with sap.

"That one's too green," he says. The fact seems to sadden him.

"Yeah," Toby says. "Fireworks!"

"It was sort of hard to see in the dark," I say defensively.

"If it's hard to break, it's probably too green," my father explains. His mind seems to be elsewhere. He shifts his eyes as if they're tired and he can't find a place to let them rest.

"Aren't any of you gentlemen going to compliment me on my fried chicken?" My father and Toby look over at Peggy Landis guiltily to see whether she's going to sulk, but I know she's smiling, her eyes dancing.

"Even better than The Colonel, Aunt Peggy," Toby assures her.

"Honey, hey, it was delicious. You know how we feel about your chicken. Can't you tell by the way we gobble it up?"

"Well, I'd just like to hear you say so once in a blue moon."

I can see that she's joking so I lick my fingers speculatively, with the superior air of a connoisseur making a pronouncement. "Not the worst I've ever had. Really quite tasty actually, yes, quite."

The English accent acts like a cue. She bows from the waist and says in a broad drawl: "Why thank you, kind sir. How very gallant indeed—"

Toby snickers. "James sounds like a fairy—"

Peggy Landis claps a hand to her mouth in mock alarm. "Such language, such language! Why, Mr. Tobias, I'm surprised at you!"

Toby is momentarily confused. He points a finger at me, shifting the blame as I have taught him to do. "What about James? He's the one that talked that way." Toby hates to be teased, he wants things to be just what they seem, like rocks and trees and the hard ground itself. Perhaps because of me, he distrusts words—they always seem to trip him up or give him the slip. I'm sure he doesn't even know what a fairy is.

My father shares some of Toby's confusion. Any reference to sex, no matter how innocent or veiled, tends to make him uncomfortable. "Okay, okay, you guys, it's been a long day, how 'bout some marshmallows for dessert and then to bed?"

"To bed?" I'm incredulous. "It's only about eight o'clock."

"Nine-thirty, as a matter of fact," Peggy Landis says in an unequivocal, somewhat flattened tone of voice. "I'll get the marshmallows and then it's time for bed, my fine-feathered friends." She stands up and the firelight undulates in waves on her bare legs, her phosphorescent shorts. The three of us stare up at her reverently for a moment. We all look a little feverish, our eyes dark or glinting in the pulsating light.

An hour later, I'm lying in our pup tent beside Toby listening to the regular, surflike rhythm of his breathing in the dark. I can always count on Toby to fall asleep almost as soon as his head touches the pillow. He sleeps the deep sleep of innocence, but I'm wide awake, waiting for something I don't even have to think about. I know without knowing. There are no fireflies or crickets yet, no nighttime kazoo chorus of tree frogs and cicadas, just the occasional purl of Peggy Landis's voice from the other side of our clearing and, from somewhere nearby, the musical trilling of some spring bird. A mockingbird, I decide; inconsistent and varied, it has no single song but a sequence that seems inexhaustible. I've heard of nightingales and wonder if this is what they sound like.

Then, as if I'd come to the end of a page and were turning over to read the next one, I peel my unzipped sleeping bag open and begin quietly inching backward on my elbows. In a moment my head is out of the tent and I'm looking up at pinpricks of starlight in the ragged hole of sky our clearing makes in the leafy black silhouette that surrounds us. When I'm all the way out, I turn over and rise to my knees. Over the bright red embers of our campfire, I can see a steady glow of light through the green walls of their tent, though of course from here I can't see inside. But inside my pajama bottoms I'm already throbbing. There is the arrow of my compass: I have only to follow.

I start crawling to the left, toward the line of the other tent's entrance, but the pine needles and stones soon hurt my knees and I realize I can probably move more quietly on the pads of my bare feet. So, hunched over like a man with a deviated sacrum, I move first to the edge of the clearing, then circle slowly clockwise from the trunk of one tree to the trunk of the next, until I'm directly opposite the front of their tent.

One flap is down, but my heart starts beating like a bird against a window when I see that the other is tied back, leaving a large, oblong

opening through which light falls in a white shaft, illuminating the
knuckles of root and, just at the edge of darkness, a lichened sitting-
stone shaped like a gigantic egg. With delicate, calculated steps I work
my way gradually forward until I'm crouched just behind this oval
stone, less than fifteen feet from the entrance. Oddly, the view inside
still seems somehow gauzy and unclear. Then I realize that the mosquito screen is down. I remember Peggy Landis's inordinate fear of
insects and feel suddenly ashamed of myself for lurking out here in the
dark and spying on people who trust me, whose fears and vulnerabili-
ties I am simply too familiar with for what I have in mind. My compass
arrow wavers, and for a moment I feel lost. Then, as my eyes begin to
decipher the shadowy forms moving behind the fine hatchwork of
screen, desire breathes on me once more and I'm just as suddenly
inspired and blooming with it all over again. Seen through the tiny
interstices of the mosquito netting, the figures in the tent are rendered
with a surreal, hallucinatory precision and at the same time thrown into
a kind of antique, pointillist distortion. At first I'm only aware of a
slow, rocking movement of light and shadow and the pallid, pinkish
glow of naked skin. I know it is happening, I know this is it, but in my
urgency I'm unable to make it out. The screen baffles my focus and the
images blur into abstraction, their personalities dissolving until they
are merely bodies moving through a dream. So it's the net that returns
the fantasy to me again, as if it has captured desire like a great glistening fish and brought it up from the depths, dripping and bright, into the
breathable air of the real. Perhaps what confuses me too is the fact that
I'm looking at them head-on and can therefore see only the dark tops of
their heads, knobs of elbow and shoulder and, beyond that, a glimpse
of what seem, in the foreshortening of my perspective, to be breasts but
which turn out to be cleft buttocks lifting and falling in the rhythm of
the moving shadows thrown by the turned-down Coleman lantern beside them. In my absorption I forget even to wonder that they're not
doing it in the dark. But this violation of modesty somehow makes me
feel vindicated. The light gives the scene an aura of spectacle, and what
am I but the necessary spectator, implicitly called for by this spot-
lighted performance?

It's at this point, just as I'm beginning to feel sure of myself and
what it is I'm watching, that the whole geography of my assumptions

shifts again. I realize that the one on top is not my father but Peggy Landis. She has pushed herself upright and sits straddling the figure beneath her, riding it. I can see perfectly the pointed brown nipples standing out from the heavy sway of her breasts. No, it's not Peggy Landis at all but someone in a photograph, someone in a dream. She leans back on her outstretched arms, letting her head fall backward so that I can no longer even see her face. I'm aware suddenly that I'm making a high-pitched, keening sound and I try to stop it but I can't. The sound is not coming from me, it's coming from inside the tent. It's unearthly. I don't know who these people are. They're fucking, I tell myself unbelievingly. I repeat the word in an effort to grasp the enormous fact, but it's too much for me, the pieces of the puzzle fly apart: my father, "Aunt" Peggy Landis, these strange coupled bodies frozen in shadowy, rocking motion, the words in my head, and, from inside the tent, a hissing, groaning sound that only gradually resolves itself into the voice of Peggy Landis. "Oh, Jesus . . . oh, Jesus," she's repeating in a kind of terrible, Pentecostal awe.

What, after all, do we really know of one another? Perhaps deep down everyone is someone else. In school we used to make jokes about knowing a person "in the biblical sense." I have a specific memory of Albie Blythe in the fifth grade leaning across the aisle, his eyes glued to the rear end of a new substitute teacher who was writing a math problem on the blackboard, and whispering: "Hey, James, how'd you like to get to *know* that Miss Rosenberg?" From very early on, that is, sex stood for the penetration of mystery. We were simply hungry for true knowledge—not so much for what we were taught (most of which seemed beside the point, an elaborate irrelevance it was necessary for some reason we get by heart) but for what we were forbidden to know. That was where life, our own lives included, really came from. And after what I had witnessed that night, I knew it was true. But as a consequence of this new knowledge, I felt as if I no longer knew my own father—although, in his case, what I had seen was somehow easier to accept than it was in hers. I don't know why this should have been so. I rarely imagined my father's sexuality, whereas I brooded constantly and energetically on the sexual gifts I imagined Peggy Landis might bestow. Maybe that was it: I had never imagined her as *taking* pleasure but only as giving it, or as merely being aware that it was hers to give. I may have imagined her as sexually conscious, even subtly and preternaturally so, but now she seemed to be someone else entirely. I realized for the first time, I think, that other people had selves that were as secret, as powerful, and as labyrinthine as my own. And in the aftermath of that discovery everything became suddenly unreal. Because now it was all a lie—clothes and good manners and conversation, Sunday school and hiking in the woods, the various rituals and formalities of relationship—it had all been canceled out by what I'd discovered in the lantern light, canceled by that frozen contortion of flesh and that unearthly hiss and groan I can still hear the echo of. There was the Peggy Landis of exaggerated Southern gentility and then there was this other one in the tent groaning the name of our Savior while she rode my father's thrusting hips—and I was lost somewhere in the gulf between the two.

I've been watching her all day—whenever she's not looking; otherwise, I'm afraid to meet her eyes. I'm trying to get a clue. The night before hardly seems real anymore. The morning was blue and sunny. We rowed out on the lake, casting unsuccessfully for perch in the shivering reflection of the sky. In the afternoon it clouded up, but we went for a long hike anyway—back in the deep woods behind the lake, then up to the fire station and back around by the park ranger's office. We have the whole park almost entirely to ourselves. It's a little eerie, like an empty house that might be haunted. Once, we heard a radio playing rock-and-roll through the trees, but we didn't see anyone and gradually the sound faded and disappeared. It's Toby's habit to carry a compass and always keep us informed of the precise direction we're moving in. He and my father mark our passage in pencil on a relief map of the park so we know exactly how high we are, where we're going and where we've been. My style is to pretend that we're lost, desperately searching for signs of civilization with no guide but intuition and our own wits. Peggy Landis picks flowers and notices birds that none of us can even see. I usually like to take the lead, but today I lagged behind so I could watch them and maybe see the connection between all this and the other. But, so far as I can tell, there is none.

It's raining now. Or it might be the wind shaking water from the trees. The raindrops make a constant but irregular patter on the tent. Again, I'm lying awake waiting. Toby has been asleep for some time. He's lying on his side with his back to me, so when I decide to move I have no trouble taking the poncho from where it lies folded next to his feet or unbuttoning the tent flap—besides, the rain covers any noise I might make. I even put on my sneakers this time.

I'm not electrified and charged with heat the way I was last night; in fact, I'm shivering. If I don't grit my teeth they'll chatter. It's a lot darker tonight. No stars, and their tent is unlit. My eyes are already adjusted to the dark, but I still have to pause and orient myself. I pull the black poncho over my shoulders and nod the hood forward. I want the feeling of protection it gives even more than I want to keep my head dry. I crouch here in the rain for a moment—looking, it occurs to me, like a superhero or a witch in my hooded cape—and then I begin moving to the left. Nearly every step finds a puddle, and before I reach the sitting-stone my sneakers are soaked. The tent seems to be closed up tight. A steady rivulet is running down a furrow from its peak into the narrow drainage ditch that encircles it like a moat. I remember that there's a small rectangle of screen, a sort of window, at the back, and I step cautiously around in that direction, moving closer to the tent at the same time.

All at once I'm aware of voices and I freeze, listening, intent as stone. The voices are mixed up with the splash of water, but I immediately catch a serious, stricken undertone. I'm unable to make out individual words and phrases, but I'm sure someone is crying, though it might be only the rainfall. No birds are singing tonight; there's just this constant drizzle, punctuated by loud spatterings from the trees whenever the wind blows. I move closer still, until I'm crouching right beside the rain trench, nearly touching the wet wall of the tent. I'm straining to hear, my head bowed as if in prayer and water dripping from the black rim of my hood like some private cloudburst all my own, when I hear Peggy Landis's voice, suddenly clear and unmuffled: ". . . still can't believe it . . . God . . . oh, God. . . ." I feel a momentary surge of excitement, thinking maybe they're doing it again, but no, almost immediately I hear fragments of my father's lower, more muted voice, his tone heavy and consolatory: ". . . you know it's . . . there's nothing . . . just have to. . . ." The words rise and drop in and out of intelligibility before becoming finally only a rhythmic, murmuring cadence that goes on and on until Peggy Landis's voice breaks through one last time, tremulous and disconsolate but lifting into perfect clarity for a moment before falling back into indecipherability and then silence, the sawing of the wind, sigh of leaves rustling, rain-spatter: ". . . goddamned doctors . . . it under control . . . he's so young . . . how can . . . it's not fair . . . just not fair. . . ." *He's so young:* these are the words I'm left with. Crouching here in the dark, I feel emptied and washed clean, even relieved somehow by what I've heard, though I know that something is profoundly, unimaginably wrong. I'm caught in a terrible drift, as if I'm being moved smoothly out and away from shore by a black tide, out and out and never coming back. As the voices fade, deep inside me I feel certain that I know, have always known, what this is all about. It's like a dark room down in the cellar of myself: the door might be closed, but I know it's there, I even know what's inside. I feel an overwhelming flood of grief. The room is my own heart, and when the door opens, it all rushes out like a river of smoke and I know that Toby is going to die.

The next day was Sunday. If it had been summer, we would have gone to the outdoor church service held on benches in a clearing just a short walk down the road. A plump, gray-haired woman with sharp eyes that looked directly out at you from behind an antique pair of rimless spectacles, always wearing what my father called her Sunday-go-to-meeting dress, would pull on a cord that ascended straight into a huge old oak to where, if you looked up, you'd see there was a cast-iron bell braced on a smooth beam of wood between two thick branches. When she pulled the cord, the bell would swing up, and then, when she released it, fall back again, tolling three clear syllables in a fading, dactylic pattern that never varied from phrase to phrase or from week to week. But that Sunday the services hadn't started yet, so we couldn't go. Instead, we spent an hour trying to build a fire with damp wood, finally giving up and using the collapsible stove and a can of Sterno to make a special breakfast of flapjacks, fried eggs, and maple syrup. It wasn't raining anymore but the sky was completely blank, shedding that diffused, muted light in which everything stands out stark and devoid of shadow or reflection. When I try to recall exactly how I felt that morning, it's that light I mostly remember. I thought I knew all the secrets now—I was the spectator who thought he knew how all the tricks were done. And I no longer wondered about anything except the incredible emptiness behind it all. Watching my father show off his skill with the frying pan, successfully flipping a pancake and then catching it perfectly flat, or watching Toby devour his flapjacks and eggs, I could see only wreckage and smoke. If yesterday I knew that the world of ordinary social life was nothing but a lie, today my wisdom went even deeper, all the way down beneath the foundations of appetite itself to where there was only empty space and silence. I had reached that bottom of certainty which is even beyond tears. After breakfast I went through the motions of striking camp with the others, packing the car, throwing dirt over the fire, going back for the water bag we'd left hanging from the tree. Then, during the long ride home, I lay suspended, my head rocking against the window while I pretended to sleep and thought about nothing.

The discovery that I was wrong came so gradually I can't even be sure of when it finally arrived. I do remember weeks of trying to make Toby forgive me—forgive us all, really. For what, I didn't even try to figure out. I just accepted it as inevitable that it would be Toby, not me, who was going to pay for what had been a kind of deliverance, after all, a release of desire that would somehow carry him off like a flake of ash rising on a current of heat into the darkness above our campfire that spring night in the woods. So, while I waited for my father to make the death sentence official, I treated Toby as if every day might be his last, letting him have the extra piece of lemon sponge pie or angel food cake, watching "The Waltons" with him, even helping him design a tree house I secretly knew he'd probably never live long enough to finish. These concessions may seem small enough (and I suppose they were), but the truth is that Toby had become real to me for the first time—real, I think, just because he was finally present to my imagination. His interests, his likes and dislikes, however ordinary they might have been, were rendered extraordinary to me by the simple knowledge that he was going to die.

In a sense, I realize now, it hardly matters that I was wrong. And in some deeper way, maybe I wasn't. It wasn't Toby who was dying after all—it was Peggy Landis's father, down among the citrus groves of sunny central Florida. Two months later she went south to be with him during his last days. She stayed several weeks, making arrangements for his burial and seeing to the various legalities connected with his estate, and when she returned things weren't the same between her and my father anymore. The first time I saw her after she got back I recognized the strange sort of tightness she'd get around her lips whenever she had to do something she didn't like. I was looking out the big picture window over the sofa because I'd heard a car drive up, and when I saw who it was I wondered why she wasn't parking in the garage the way she usually did. Then I saw that funny expression around her mouth and knew that something was wrong. Just tired after the long trip, she said. But it was more than that: she'd come by to tell us she and her mother were going back to Florida for good. And less than a month later she was gone. Maybe she'd met someone else down there—I'm not sure. I tried to find out from my father, but if he ever knew he never talked about it.

In August, nearly a year after she moved away, she sent me a catcher's mitt for my fourteenth birthday. It was an odd gift because I've never been very athletic. Toby's always been the athlete in the family, as she surely must have known. He might have used it himself, except he'd always rather pitch than catch. For a long time it sat on the top of my dresser, propped up against the wall like a photograph or a fishing trophy. For some reason I liked to look at the oversized, abstract shape of it: a huge hand without fingers and a permanent pocket into which the ball of my fist fit with the satisfactory snugness of something that has found its natural groove—the way a road map can fold in upon itself like a solved puzzle, all its outspread sections falling so neatly and reassuringly back into place that for a moment it's hard to believe you could ever really be lost.

Coming Unbalanced

When I found Blanco he was sitting in a circle of sunlight in the clearing out behind the cabin. Eyes closed, chin lifted, he looked like he was listening to something, but I couldn't tell what. From where I was standing, all I could hear was a truck changing gears out on the highway, a big semi, you could tell, downshifting into low, just starting up the long grade. The noon air was still and heavy, even back here in the woods where there was usually a little breeze blowing, moving the shadows of the high pine branches around so that pieces of sunlight were always dancing under your feet. I could hear a yellow jacket buzzing close to my ear and I waved my hand to keep it from getting any closer.

"Blanco?" I said. But he didn't hear me. I thought maybe I hadn't actually said anything, or if I had maybe the heat had swallowed it up. The spokes and the metal rims of Blanco's wheelchair were shimmering in the sunlight. They looked too hot to touch, and the fuzzy nest of pale reddish hair that grew above Blanco's ears and circled back under the great shiny egg of his bald head was glowing too, as if his chair were really the famous electric one itself and Blanco was sizzling his way to heaven right at that very moment. A gone-to-glory look was on his face, even if my sister Candace never tired of telling him to go to hell. The road to hell was paved with good intentions, she said, and in a voice that sounded like he was reading out loud with no one to listen but himself, Blanco'd say, "Roadwork, my sweet Candy Cane, of which I am sure you will never be accused." "You can go straight to hell," Candace would say. "Do not pass Go, do not collect two hundred dollars." Blanco would smile his smile and say, "Where else but?" He'd sweep his arms out over the big wheels of the chair, his muscles bulging, his hands open palms up, and he'd say, "Where else but here? Here where the heart is?" Candace might slam a cupboard door if she was in the kitchen, or bang down her can of diet soda on top of the TV set if she'd been trying to get the picture to stand still, and then she'd stamp outside and the next thing we'd hear would be the car starting up and her peeling out through the trees, scattering what gravel there was left and digging the ruts even deeper into the driveway that Blanco kept telling her he'd have to hire someone to fix before too long. After she was gone, he'd move his chair over to the window, spinning the wheels with just a touch of his long fingers, his hands poised flat at the top of each metal rim. The chair would glide without a sound, spokes glinting and blurring as the wheels revolved. He'd look out the window at the dust she'd raised as it settled in the driveway or at raindrops sliding down the pane, and over his shoulder he'd say to me, "Here we go again, pardner, here we go again."

This time was different though. This time I hadn't heard any argument at all. I'd taken Blanco's car into town to pick up the mail and run a few errands. I was feeling fidgety because school would be starting again in a couple of weeks and I was wondering how I'd ever get the money together for a second year of college, much less a third and a fourth. When I got back to the cabin, Candace's suitcases were already packed. She was throwing the rest of her stuff into a cardboard box when I walked in. It took me a little by surprise; I'd been staying with them all summer—after school let out in May I hadn't had anyplace else to go—but I'd never actually seen her move out before. "What's going on?" I asked, but all she'd say was, "Ask him—the bastard."

Now I was standing in the path that led from the back porch through black raspberry vines and scrub brush to the graveled clearing where Blanco liked to chop kindling, which he did right from his wheelchair, lifting the heavy mallet high over his head and coming down square on the wedge. Blanco had been in and out of a wheelchair for two of the three years he and Candace had known each other, and the doctors still couldn't agree on exactly what was wrong. Some said he had multiple sclerosis and told him to stay out of the sun; others called it spinal demyelinization and suggested that the disease might vanish as suddenly as it had come. In the meantime, Blanco was spending his days reading Shakespeare and chopping wood. He'd taken an extended leave of absence from the university where he taught and retreated here to the log cabin he'd inherited from his mother's father. He said the woods were the only place he'd ever truly felt at home. After Vietnam, he'd even worked as a professional climber for a few years before getting his Ph.D. A climber is a man who climbs up into a tree and cuts it down in sections from the top. According to Blanco, you had to be part Indian and a little nuts to be a first-rate climber, and Blanco claimed to be one-quarter Chickasaw on his mother's side and half crazy on his father's. Resin ran in his blood, he said, and it's true that he split kindling the way another man might crack his knuckles or smoke cigarettes. He certainly had more firewood than he'd likely ever use. It was stacked in neat cords under a tin roof roped to the trunks of four tall pines, the cords arranged just inside the roof's perimeter, like a kid's fort. The clearing was on a little rise and Blanco had made the walls high enough so you couldn't see him when he was in there. All you'd be able to see, and then only if you looked pretty hard, would be the wisp of white smoke from the joint he'd be smoking. He wasn't in the fort when I found him this time, he was sitting out in the sun, but the look on his face told me he'd already taken his little trip to the woodpile.

"Blanco?" I said again. When he didn't answer, I knew he'd heard me the first time. "Why's Candace packing her bags?" I said. "What's going on?"

Blanco pivoted the chair until he faced me. His brow knit and his lips pursed the way they do when you bite into something sour, but he still didn't say anything. Instead, he pivoted away and pointed himself back in the direction he'd been pointing in when I came up. Then I saw what he'd been meditating on. I knew what it was in a second—don't ask me how, I'd only ever seen it once before. I'd been going through Candace's drawers looking for one of the T-shirts she was always borrowing, and I'd come across a blue plastic case, flat and oval, with a scalloped lid that was curved like an oyster shell. The case had been in

Candace's lingerie drawer, nestled in among a lot of glossy nylon and
elasticized lace, and when I opened it up I'd found a rubbery, flesh-
colored diaphragm inside, just like the one now lodged at about shoulder height in the rough bark of an oak tree on the edge of the clearing. I
was wondering what it might mean when I saw Blanco's hand rise up
from the other side of his chair and level the .22 pistol he kept for rats
and dangerous snakes. There was a sudden snapping sound and when I
looked back at the tree I could see that he'd hit the little rubber circle
dead center. Blanco was a crack shot.

"Jesus, Blanco, what're you doing?"

"Little target practice," Blanco said. "Breathing and concentration.
You could say that the separation of subject and object is a Cartesian
illusion I am working hard to dissolve." He raised the pistol and fired
again, this time spinning the diaphragm away from the tree like a
flipped coin. Blanco must have thought the same thing I did, because
he turned to me and said, "Heads or tails, pardner? You call it." He
laughed a harsh laugh and pretended to blow smoke from the barrel of
his .22, a six-shooter styled to look like a Colt .45, the gun, Blanco
liked to say, that blessed the West. He put the pistol in his lap and
wheeled himself along one of the plywood tracks he'd laid down out
here to make wheeling easier. When he came to where the diaphragm
had fallen, he leaned over and picked it up, then sat back and twirled it
on the tip of his finger. "Just thought your sister might need help
packing, is all. You know, make sure she gets everything she deserves.
Then it occurred to me she might like a little something to remember
me by, maybe a medallion to wear around her pretty little neck." He
held the diaphragm encircled by his thumb and forefinger now, as if he
were giving me the high sign with it, saying, Aces, pard, don't worry
'bout a thing.

"So what if she's leaving," I told him. "She'll be back. Like a bad
penny. We both know that."

"So we do, so we do," Blanco said. "But I am holding in my hand
precisely what I did not know. These holes could be said to represent
my fall into knowledge, a sort of immaculate conception you might
even say, oh Jesus, yes, oh Jesus—" He pivoted away from me and
sailed the thing backhand. It arced across the clearing like a tiny Fris-
bee and landed with a thunk out of sight on the tin roof of Blanco's

firewood fort. "Goddamn it to hell," Blanco said. "Goddamn it to bloody hell."

Candace was hanging up the wall phone when I came into the kitchen through the screen door.

"My God, you'd think I was his teenage daughter," she said. "Or else his holy wedded wife. Which I would be, too, if he weren't so worried about his precious bank account. Just tell him that the next time he starts calling me names, blaming everything on me—" Blanco's family was oil rich. He'd inherited enough money to live off nothing but the interest for the rest of his life, but he was already paying alimony to one ex-wife, and Candace believed he saw another marriage, at least to her, as a threat to his financial independence. "He doesn't own me," she said. "We are both free agents—that's the way he wanted it, that's the way it is."

Candace was talking fast but she was keeping her voice quiet. Instead of yelling, she kept moving, taking a drag of her cigarette then clutching her elbows across her chest and striding from the phone to the sink, turning, opening the refrigerator door but only glancing in before closing it again, going back to the sink, picking up a green tomato from a row of five sitting on the windowsill then setting it back down, filling a glass half full of water and swirling it as she turned around. This was the sort of nervous dance Candace always did whenever she felt backed into a corner, which happened more often than you'd think given the fact that Candace was such an expert at cornering the other guy, whether it was me or Blanco or some perfect stranger. I didn't know how well my father would've made out if he'd hung around, but when my mother was alive she used to treat Candace like she was handling high explosives, as if all you had to do was sneeze at the wrong moment and Candace might blow us all to kingdom come.

She held the glass of water up to the light, watching the little bubbles rise to the surface, then she took one small sip and splashed the rest out. "I'm outta here, kiddo," she said. "I'll send you a postcard from Timbuktu."

"Who was that on the phone just now?"

"Nobody you'd know. A friend. He's coming to pick me up. If we didn't live so far out in the sticks, I'd've called a cab."

Candace always seemed to have some guy off on the sidelines some-where just waiting to try his luck. There was a time when it used to make me so jealous I'd actually get sick thinking about it, back in the days when she was still using me to practice on, petting over me all the time, even sneaking into my bed one unbelievable night when I was thirteen because she said there were some things I ought to know about—then going on to show me in detail, but just that once, probably figuring after that I was hers to keep—and she was right, for a long time I was.

"Yeah, it must be real tough," I said. "Out here in the sticks and all. Poor little you, right?"

She gave me a quick, injured look. "Don't make it any harder, Mi-key, please—you don't know anything about it—" She brushed a hand across her forehead and tossed a wing of hair over her shoulder, first one side, then the other. Her hair was brown, long and straight and streaked with highlights from her squeezing lemon juice on it and lying in the sun. Her arms and legs had darkened almost to the color of copper. She was wearing a sleeveless yellow jersey, faded cut-offs with a tiny yellow flower she'd painted on the left thigh, and no shoes. Although Candace liked to throw shoes, she hardly ever wore them.

We heard the buckling sound of the plywood ramp to the porch and then the screen door opened and there was Blanco. "On second thought," he said, "let's just forget it. I'm sorry I ever found the god-damn thing. You want a little on the side, you've got a perfect right to it—who am I to say you nay? Hell, I ought to be glad you're being so careful."

"Ow!" Candace yelled. She dropped the smoking stub of her ciga-rette, shook her hand for a second, and stuck two fingers in her mouth.

"Run cold water on it," Blanco said. "Forget butter. That's out—like everything else our mothers told us." Leaning over, he picked the smol-dering butt up off the floor and pinched the tip.

Candace had taken her fingers out of her mouth and was examining the burned place. "Damn it," she said. "There's already a blister." She turned the faucet on, extended her middle finger, and strummed the stream of water in a vaguely obscene way with her fingertip, twitching it back and forth and flinging off droplets like sparks.

"No need to jump into anything here," Blanco said. "Or out of anything either. Let's use our heads for a minute."

"Your head, you mean—let's use your head, isn't that right, Blanco? Isn't that what always happens?"

"Christ, my head's just about all I've got left, don't take that away from me too—"

"I'm not taking anything away from you. I'm only trying to figure out what's mine and what isn't. And I suggest you do the same. For instance, here's one thing I figured out—what you took was most assuredly mine and not yours."

"Most assuredly not," Blanco said, and then with a trace of the Irish brogue he affected along with his cowboy twang, "but I'm afraid I no longer have it in me possession to return." He smiled and nodded in my direction. "Ask me old pard Michael there if you don't believe me. B'gorra, the bloody thing up and flew away like a bird."

"Blanco, you are so full of bullshit it's a wonder you don't attract flies," Candace said. She was drying her hand gingerly on a flowered dish towel, first dabbing at the hurt finger, then sucking on it.

"I guess flies are more attracted to candy, honey love," Blanco said. "Especially flies with zippers, what?"

"Oh, you bastard," Candace said. "You son of a bitch."

"There, there," Blanco said. " 'What, sweeting, all amort?' "

"I'm all amort, all right," Candace said, her voice steady and self-possessed. "I'm all amort out of here for good in about five minutes. No kidding this time, Blanco. I've really had it." She carefully folded the dish towel and hung it neatly on the rack behind the sink, a way of declaring how different this time was from all the temper tantrums she'd thrown before.

"Listen," Blanco said in an earnest tone. "Michael, tell her. It was an accident, that's all, what was I supposed to do? I didn't even know it was in there—I mean I wasn't snooping around in your purse, I was looking for an Excedrin. That's the God's honest truth. Jesus, listen to me, now you've got *me* on the defensive, and I didn't do anything. Michael, you tell her—"

I'd been sitting at the kitchen table through all this trying to balance the glass salt shaker on edge against a single grain of salt. I'd seen

Blanco do it a hundred times, just by touch, but somehow I could never get it to work. I spilled some more salt and tried again. "Leave me out of this," I said. "As long as she leaves the car, I'm staying neutral."

"The car," Candace said. "The goddamned car. I've got to get out of here before I go crazy too." She turned around and walked into the living room.

"Don't worry," I called after her. "You've got to be sane first to go crazy." I looked over at Blanco, but he was watching Candace through the doorway.

"How're you going to carry all that stuff if you don't take the car?" he asked her.

Instead of an answer, there was the sound of something heavy sliding across the hardwood floor, then the sound of the screen door to the front porch slamming shut.

Blanco turned toward me with a slightly pop-eyed look. "Someone's picking her up, is that it? She's being picked up, isn't she? I bet she planned the whole thing from the start. She knew I'd find the goddamned diaphragm because she planted it—"

"She was on the phone when you were out back playing cowboy," I said. "But Candace doesn't plan things, you know that, she just does them." I looked down to where I held the salt shaker tilted but still unbalanced among the spilled crystals. A slight adjustment and I felt the shaker's bevelled bottom edge find a sort of foothold and come to rest. I took my fingers away and the salt shaker stood by itself, pitched over at a forty-five-degree angle in apparent defiance of gravity. When I blew away the excess salt, the shaker stayed where it was as if by special dispensation, held up by absolutely nothing you could see.

"There, listen," Blanco said. "Hear that? It's a car, somebody's coming up the driveway. What the hell's going on around here?" he shouted at Candace. "I'm supposed to be the one leaving you, god-damnit, not the—you didn't find *my* diaphragm, I'm not the adulterer, *you* are—Christ, you've got me sounding like Roger Chillingworth, this is insane—"

He went wheeling into the living room, moving out of my line of vision as he talked. For just a moment, I sat in the kitchen by myself, studying the fine unlikely sight of a half-filled salt shaker standing tipped over on one edge, miraculously untumbled, and then I carefully extricated myself from the table and went after him.

I hadn't forgotten about the .22, but I wasn't considering it seriously either. Blanco sometimes used words as if they were knives, I mean he could lacerate and flay you with them, but I'd never seen him do anything you could really call violent. He liked to make gestures, that's all. He liked to express himself. Shooting holes through Candace's diaphragm meant not having to shoot holes through *her.* I understood that, but I was still wondering what he'd done with the .22—I didn't think he'd leave it outside.

Candace was just coming back in from the porch as I came into the living room from the kitchen. "I'll write you a letter," she said to me. "You can stay here until we figure something out."

"Great," I said. "Is that it? 'I'll write you a letter,' 'we'll figure something out'? Where're you going? What about me?"

"I'll let you know."

Blanco was sitting transfixed, staring out through the screen door. Out in the parking area about thirty yards away, next to where Blanco's old Subaru sedan was drawn up to its plywood dock, stood a mud-spattered, olive-green Jeep Pioneer painted in the random jigsaw patterns of camouflage.

"My God," Blanco said. "The Marines have landed."

The Jeep door swung open and a heavyset bearded man stepped out. He stood there craning his neck at the cabin, evidently unsure of what to do next. He hardly looked like Candace's type. With his chino shorts and brown knee socks, he could have been a Scout leader who'd lost his compass. He lifted the billed cap he was wearing and wiped the back of his hand across his forehead. "Candace?" he called. "Need any help?"

"That son of a bitch is not coming up here," Blanco said.

Candace turned to me. "Michael, come on. There's a box of my things out on the porch. If you get that, I can carry these two suitcases myself."

"Whatever," I said. "Let's just get it over with."

When Candace and I came out onto the porch, the man was already walking toward the cabin. "How was that for quick time?" he called out.

"Wait there, Phil," Candace said in a bright, commanding voice. "I'll be right down."

She stood holding the suitcases and facing out toward the trees. Her jeans were cut to less than an inch below her back pockets and fringed with frayed little tufts of white thread. "Blanco?" she said without turning around. When he didn't answer, she shook her head, hefted her bags to get a better grip and stepped down off the porch.

I was about to follow with the cardboard box when Blanco came out through the screen door. He was holding the pistol in his lap and he was wearing his cold mask of a smile.

"This won't do," he said. "I've got a gun here, so everybody just freeze."

I'd heard so many variations of that line in the movies my first reaction was to laugh, but when I looked at Blanco I could tell he wasn't joking. Candace could tell too—she'd come to a sudden halt. "I think maybe this is a bad idea," I told Blanco. "That cowboy gun's for real."

"Real enough," Blanco said. "Barring niceties of metaphysical dispute. As real anyway as this ridiculous dream we're stuck in." Keeping his elbow on the wheelchair's armrest, he raised the pistol off his lap and casually held it in the air. "Maybe this'll wake us all up," he said, then he called out, "What do you say, compadre, doesn't this make you feel more awake?" He waved the six-gun and smiled that damn know-it-all smile.

Phil was still standing where Candace had told him to wait. He'd been fanning the air with his cap, but now he cupped it to his ear. "Do I what?" he asked.

Candace set her bags down and turned around. "Don't do this, Blanco. Please, don't do this."

"Why not?" Blanco said. "I feel better already. I'm doing exactly what I want to. All the things we tell ourselves we can't do, but what if you just go ahead and give yourself permission? Isn't that your way, Candy? Just say do instead of don't?"

"Here, let me give you a hand with that stuff," Phil called. He started forward, still waving at the air with his cap. "Dad-blasted mosquitoes," he said.

"It's okay, Phil," Candace told him. "Get back in the Jeep."

Phil stopped, looked at each of us in turn, and shrugged his shoulders. He gave the air a final swat with his cap before tugging it back on. "I'll just wait in the Jeep," he said. "It's not so buggy in there." He walked back to the camouflaged Pioneer and climbed inside.

"Come on, Blanco," I said. "Give it up. What's the use?"

"An arresting argument, Michael, but a young man your age should be more hopeful. Like your big sister there."

Candace wasn't even looking at the gun. She had her eyes locked on Blanco's. "Please," she said. "We can talk it all out some other time."

"No more talk, honeychile, it's time for action now. I can do what I feel like, too. See?" He pointed the gun and before I could move or even yell he fired it. There was an instant when I thought he was aiming at Candace—some buried, sickening part of me actually leaping at the idea—but then I heard one of Phil's headlights pop, almost like a flashbulb going off.

"Blanco, you crazy bastard," Candace screamed. She whirled around at him, and at the same moment Phil came scrambling out of his Jeep. I put down the box so I'd have my hands free in case I thought of anything to do. Blanco was laughing, not maniacally, just softly chuckling. He lowered the gun to get a grip on his wheelchair, so he could move out of Candace's way if he had to, and when he did the gun went off again. "Sweet Jesus Mother of Christ," Blanco said with an astonished look on his face. "I think I've shot myself in the foot."

All four of us were in the oversized Jeep, Candace and me in the back, Blanco sitting in the front next to Phil. There was a clean hole in the top of Blanco's right shoe, just beneath the laces and slightly off center toward the little toe, but the bullet hadn't come out the other side. There wasn't a mark on the sole, and there didn't appear to be any bleeding either—not very good signs, according to Phil, who turned out to be an anesthesiologist. The best thing, he said, was not to touch the shoe, keep the foot raised, and get to the hospital immediately, which is what we were trying to do. The strange part was that because of his paralysis, Blanco couldn't feel any pain.

"I guess it sounds funny to say so," Phil said, "but you're damn lucky. If it weren't for the paralysis, the internal bleeding would have

that foot throbbing to beat the band by now. As it is, you don't have
to worry."

"That's real good to know, Phil," Blanco said. "Puts my mind right
at ease." He sat as Phil had arranged him after we'd lifted him in, the
foot with the hole in it propped up on his left knee so he looked oddly
relaxed. "Hear that, everybody? Phil says it's lucky the paralysis keeps
me from feeling anything down there. Phil, did you ever read a story by
Ernest Hemingway called, 'The Snows of Kilimanjaro'? The first sentence is one of my particular favorites. It goes, 'The marvellous thing is
that it's painless,' Harry said. 'That's how you know when it starts.'
Poor old Harry dying of gangrene out there in the jungle from the mere
scratch of a thorn. Ever read that one, Phil? Right up your alley, I'd
say—all about pain and anesthesia."

"That's right," Phil said. "Candace mentioned that you're a college
professor. She told me that's how you two met."

"Did she, now?" Blanco said, turning to look over his shoulder at
Candace. "I guess you have me at a disadvantage then—she never said
a word about you."

Phil raised his eyes to the rearview mirror and then dropped them
back down again. We had just come out of the narrow mountain road
onto the highway. Four lanes wide, white asphalt instead of black mac-
adam, it cut a broad swath through the pine forest. From the highway
we could see the mountains we were in: green and blue tiers of cloud-
shadowed, densely wooded ridges that were part of the Pennsylvania
Appalachians.

"Well, let's see," Phil said. "What would you like to know?"

"I don't think what I'd *like* has a goddamned thing to do with it,"
Blanco said. "How about, how long have you been boffing my old
lady? How's that for starters?"

Candace reached over and slapped Blanco on the back of the head.
"Can't you act like a normal person once in a while?" she said. "What
do you always have to say things like that for?"

"Because I want to know the answer, that's why," Blanco said. "Is
saying things any worse than doing them?"

"I met Philip at the hospital last May when I took you in for your
physical," Candace said. "We're just friends—however hard that may
be for you to believe."

"No law against friendship, is there?" Phil said. "I mean it's not like Candace was a married woman—"

"There," Candace said with a smug look. "What did I tell you. None of this would've even happened if we'd been married—and we would be, too, if you just had a little trust instead of being so full of self-pity you could choke—"

"Come on, Candace," I said. "That's not fair—"

"Why not, I'd like to know? It's the truth."

"The truth, is it?" Blanco said. "The truth is out on top of the woodpile with two holes blasted through it. And what was it doing in your purse, anyway, if you weren't using it with Phil? If Phil's not the lucky guy, who is? Just how many aces have you got in the hole?"

Candace narrowed her eyes and her face went hard and taut. We were rounding a bend in the road and she put a hand on my leg to keep her balance, I could feel her fingernails pressing into my bare thigh. "You think you're so smart," she said, "and you don't know a goddamned thing. You want to know what you don't know? You want to know something for an absolute fact? Try this: I'm already pregnant. Ha! Try that one on for size. I'm already almost five weeks gone. And guess whose it is? Nobody else but yours, that's whose—I put that diaphragm in my purse after one of our fights just to make sure it wouldn't ever be anybody else's by mistake. But I never had to use it because there never even was anybody else." She wiped at the corner of her eye with her blistered finger. "But if you think I'm going to have your little bastard, you're crazy."

"Crazy?" Blanco said. "Crazy? What in God's name are you saying? You bought the thing *just in case?* But how can I be the father? You mean last month? That was all it took?" Back in July, Blanco'd had one of his periods of remission. He'd still been paralyzed, but for a few days sensation had returned.

Phil made a nervous, throat-clearing sound. He started to say something then changed his mind.

"Wouldn't you guys rather discuss this stuff in private?" I said, squirming in my seat. "I mean, I don't think I want to know all this."

"Of course you do, pard, of course you do," Blanco said. "This way you'll have a comeback handy whenever anybody tries to clobber you with notions about so-called real life. Because, let me tell you true, out here in the wild and woolly whatsis I promise you there ain't nothin' but dreams and nightmares—" He was twisting around, trying to look Candace in the eye. "A baby!" he yelled. "Hoo-boy!" He bent his arm around to grab my knee but he couldn't quite reach. "That makes you an uncle, old pardner, won't that be a piss?"

"Yeah, I guess," I said, trying to come up with something appropriate. "When's it due?"

"It isn't," Candace said. "I'm not having it." She was looking away from all of us, her face turned toward the side window. We'd come out of the mountains and were passing through fields thick with Queen Anne's lace and black-eyed Susans. Everything was overlush and heavy, exhausted-looking and ready for the fall.

"I guess if you just look at it as a kind of accident—," Phil began.

"I don't believe in accidents," Blanco said. "Accidents are for the superstitious. I believe there is definitely *something going on* out there. And so does Candace. Don't you, Candace?"

"What's mine is mine, that's all," Candace said. "To do with as I see fit."

"But in this case what's yours is also mine, isn't that what you're telling me?" Blanco said. "Aren't you offering the diaphragm as proof that the baby's mine and nobody else's? A logic, by the way, which absolutely defies rational thought but which does have all the earmarks of a Candy Cane original, I must admit—'always true to you, darlin', in my fashion,' isn't that the idea?"

"Stuff the idea," Candace said. "I'm not about to be the mother of your bastard, it's as simple as that."

"But Candy, it's the absolute rage. Look at Vanessa Redgrave, look at Jessica Lange. Don't you watch Donahue? An illegitimate child's nothing to be ashamed of anymore, just the opposite, such a decision shows independence of mind and reverence for life. Isn't that right, Phil? You're a doctor, tell her about reverence for life."

"Well, I don't think there's quite the same stigma attached to it there once was, that's for sure." Phil stroked his beard, mulling it over.

"What about reverence for *my* life?" Candace said. "What about a little reverence for that?"

"All the reverence in the world, Candy m'love, all the reverence in the world." Blanco suddenly reached out and grabbed hold of his wounded foot. "Ow!" he said. "That was a definite twinge of pain. My God, wouldn't it take the cake if the pain came back and I went into remission with a bullet hole in me bloody foot, God bugger it to hell— Jesus, there it goes again! I don't know if it's a phantom or not, but it hurts all the same like the bloody blue blazes— "

"Only be a minute or two now," Phil said, pulling up to a stoplight on the edge of town. "We'll have you feeling no pain in a jiffy."

"Unless it's a phantom," Blanco said. "A phantom's as real as any pain in the book, but you can't touch it 'cause it ain't there. Food for thought, *that* is, food for bloody thought— " Beside us, Howard Johnson's orange roof shimmered in the sunlight and little glimmering puddles of heat mirage played across the near-empty parking lot.

"Actually, we've got techniques for that, too," Phil said as the light turned green. "Ever try hypnosis?"

That evening, Blanco finally agreed to marry Candace, she agreed to have his baby, and I agreed to serve as best man, godfather, and general factotum. Good old Phil, who bore Blanco no grudge for his damaged headlight, stuck by us all the way. At the hospital, they'd cut off Blanco's shoe and given him a tetanus shot while we filled out a police report; they'd taken an X-ray, removed the bullet along with a few minuscule fragments of bone and shoe leather, drained the wound, then wrapped the foot up in gauze, plastic splints, and adhesive tape. In spite of medication, Blanco said the wound continued to hurt, but he was taking that as a good sign: it might mean another period of remission and, who knows, maybe the worst was over and from now on the grip of the disease would start to loosen. When we'd gotten back from the hospital, the salt shaker was still balanced where I'd left it on the kitchen table, and Blanco said that was a good sign, too.

Now, the three of them were sitting out on the front porch drinking beer in the dim, flickering light thrown by two citronella candles. For the previous hour and a half, we'd been thinking up possible names for the new kid, boys' names first and then girls' names and finally names that were increasingly outlandish, until at last I'd gotten restless and come inside. All around us the night had been pulsing with the chatter of crickets and cicadas, but at some point they'd quit and now a cool gust of breeze with the smell of rain on it came in through the open windows, riffling curtains and lifting a page of the newspaper I had spread out over Blanco's pistol on the hassock in front of me. From off somewhere among the folds of mountain to our south came the rumbling of thunder, low and prolonged and as visceral as a growl of hunger in your stomach.

" 'Bubble, bubble, toil and trouble,' " I heard Blanco say. "Storm brewin'. Oops, there go the candles—nicer in the dark, anyway—who needs light?"

"Michael, you better close the upstairs windows," Candace called. I could hear the creaking chains of the porch swing Phil was sitting on, and in the lamplight that fell through a porch window I could see one of the chrome handrails that rimmed Blanco's wheels. I folded the newspaper around the pistol and tucked it under my arm. I thought I'd better put it somewhere out of the way and safe, but I also wanted to hold on to the odd feeling of anticipation it gave me, the feeling of having some kind of choice.

Upstairs, the wind was whipping the curtains and blinds around and fluttering papers. The upstairs room was mine by default, since Blanco couldn't get to it anymore. I'd been sleeping here for the better part of three months. Blanco had put me on to Melville, and a copy of *Pierre* was lying on the floor next to the mattress I slept on. "Amidst his gray philosophizings," Melville wrote, "Life breaks upon a man like a morning." I thought that was wonderful, and I was waiting for my own morning to arrive, which it gave every sign of never doing. In the meantime, I was reading Blanco's books and treading water—literally, out at Laurel Lake. Not counting Candace, I suppose that was what Blanco and I had in common—reading books and treading water. Hundreds of paperbacks were stacked against the walls and piled on the desk and bureau. The ceiling slanted with the roof, and the dormer windows went all the way down to the floor. Part bedroom, part attic, the room was as wide as the cabin itself, with windows in every wall so it was always airy and cool, even in the deep of summer.

I knelt down and slid the folded newspaper with the pistol in it under the mattress, pushing it up against the wall at the head of the bed so the pillow would cover any possible bulge. Then I started closing windows. I'd unpropped all but one when a spasm of lightning lit the room up dead white and a crash of thunder made the boards vibrate under my feet. After the lightning flickered out, the room went pitch black. Through the open window, I could hear the rushing noise of the storm growing louder, hissing toward us through the trees. I could smell it, too, a pungent odor of ozone and dust, and then in the next instant it was here, pounding on the roof and rattling against the window panes like hail, coming down in waves, torrential sheets of it exploding off the shingles in a million tiny flashes. I closed the window, and rainwater immediately smeared across the pane, obliterating everything in sight. My face was wet with it. I licked it from my lips and wiped it from my eyes with the back of my hand. Shaking droplets from my fingers, I had an image of Candace's finger strumming across the stream of water in the sink. There was a flashlight on the floor beside my bed, and I switched it on and stood there shining the light around the room and listening to the rain. I felt vaguely excited, vaguely like a thief.

Downstairs, I went around banging windows closed, then lit two hurricane lamps and a kerosene lantern. The light they gave off was bright and steady, but with a slight pulse to it that made the shadows tremble. I was on my way into the kitchen with one of the hurricane lamps when Candace came in from the front porch. She'd been drinking beer all evening and she looked a little tipsy. When she saw me, she smiled and held a finger to her lips. "Shhh," she whispered. "Don't tell Blanco." She walked toward me, guiding herself by sliding a hand along the backs of chairs.

"Don't tell Blanco what?"

She grinned conspiratorily and stroked my cheek with the palm of her hand. "Sweet Michael," she said. "You can't tell what you don't know yet, can you?" She held her finger to her lips again and started to giggle. "Mum's the word," she said. "Get it? Mum's the word." She grabbed my arm to steady herself and the candle flame wavered inside the glass shield of the lamp I was holding. Our shadows bobbed and shifted.

"What's the joke?" I asked.

"Don't you get it? Mum's the word. I might never've even thought of it if he hadn't found the stupid diaphragm. But it'll come true, don't you worry—we'll *make* it come true, what's five weeks?"

Just then Blanco called in from the porch. "Candace? Where'd you go for chrissake? Phil says to get your ass out here—you're missing the end of the goddamn world—"

"It's only rain," Candace called back. "It makes the grass green and waters the flowers. I'm just in here with Michael getting a beer." She took a bottle out of the refrigerator and opened it up, and when she turned back around I still hadn't moved. She came up close to me then and put a hand on my shoulder. "I love you, Michael," she said. She looked me deep in the eyes, and the candle gave each of her pupils a hard little flame of sincerity. "Don't worry, baby, everything'll turn out fine. We'll all be happy, you'll see." She raised up on her toes and kissed me on the lips. Her mouth opened slightly and I could feel the tip of her tongue like a warm pearl. Then she pulled away and looked me in the eyes again. "Hmmm?" she murmured. She touched my chin with the soft pad of her finger and let the finger trail slowly down my chest. "It'll be fun," she whispered. "Remember?" Keeping her eyes locked on mine, she took a long swallow of beer, lowered the bottle, and gave me a sly grin. Then she turned and walked none too steadily back through the shadows toward the porch.

After she left, I still didn't move. I stood there feeling my pulse beat in the candlelight. At a certain moment, I set the lamp down on the counter by the sink and turned around. The salt shaker was still standing balanced on edge in the middle of the table. It reflected the candlelight and cast a long shadow that fluttered like a banner. " 'What so proudly we hailed at the twilight's last gleaming,' " I said. I laughed a sour laugh and, in spite of everything, offered it a salute. Balance was possible, the salt shaker seemed to say back: keep your balance and you can weather any storm. A neat trick, I thought. But what about when it really starts to come down? And I tapped the table edge with my finger, feeling a slight tickle of power, thinking: that's all it would take, just a little push.

for Judy Whalen, 1926–1985

Movements of the Hand

A few hours earlier, driving back to school in Illinois from my grandfather's funeral in Pennsylvania, I'd stared into the snow swirling in the headlights of the old Studebaker he'd left me and thought about all the ways a car might help me get Dana back. Men and women weren't allowed past the first floor of each other's residence halls in those days, and all winter long one of our problems had been that we had no place to go. But now we'd have the Studebaker. Dana'd agreed to come out tonight just so I could show it to her. It was a Sunday evening at the tail end of March—official spring, but snow was falling. We were parked outside Dana's sorority house, and already the car felt like a sanctuary.

"We could take a few days over spring break and drive to Florida," I said, trying to keep my voice reasonable and calm. Spring break was nearly two weeks away but I wanted to show her how patient and undesperate I could be. "No expectations of any kind," I said. "Just friends. Get away from the cold, lie in the sun—we could go all the way to Key West if we wanted to—" I had the motor running and the heater on, and the chassis vibrated as if we were already moving.

Dana stretched forward to clear a circle on the windshield with the back of her glove. Her hair was black and curly, cut short at the back and tumbling in bangs over the high curve of her forehead. She was small and fine-boned, but with a kind of defiance in the way she moved that was like a child's brave denial of vulnerability.

"Say something," I said, pushing against the steering wheel. The brake lights of the car parked in front of us came on, went off, came on again. I could see the snow drifting past a streetlight, falling on and on in a sort of slow-motion dream time that made me clench my teeth and want to break something.

"Kenny, listen," Dana said. "I like your car. I think it's great, I really do. But going to Florida, it's just not—" She paused and looked down at her lap instead of at me. "Nothing's changed. Everything we talked about . . . I mean, we agreed. Everything's been getting so serious and overwhelming lately—"

"But that's what I'm saying," I told her. "Maybe if we could just lighten the mood, be easy with each other again instead of being so gloomy all the time—because if you ask me *that's* what's killing us—"

Dana flinched. "It's not something anybody chose, though, is it?" she said in the clipped voice she got when she was angry. Her head was tilted down so her eyes were in shadow, but the other car's brake lights gave the edges of her face a faint pink glow. "My mother certainly didn't choose what's happening." When she turned to look at me her eyes glinted.

I slapped the steering wheel with the palm of my hand, then reached out and switched off the ignition. The engine went into a momentary little convulsion and all at once the car was still. Here it was, the real problem—which wasn't that I suffocated Dana with my expectations, though that's what she said, but something else entirely. It was the fact that Dana's mother was dying, and it was like a deep crevice in the ground between us, opening wider and wider, until there didn't seem to be any way to reach back across. Her mother was all the family Dana'd ever really had, and in October she'd found a lump in the heel of her right thumb that had turned out to be a particularly virulent form of lymphatic melanoma.

"I'm sorry," I said. "I didn't mean it like that. I'm talking about us, I'm talking about—" I broke off again. In the new silence of the car, my voice sounded loud and insistent. I was always having to catch myself this way, always having to pull myself in. "I'm talking about what's happening to us," I said more softly, and then, as gently as I could, "We're important, too."

Dana reached over and uncurled my right hand from the wheel. She was wearing wool gloves with a jagged light-and-dark pattern but my own hand was white-knuckled and bare. She turned it over and ran her finger along the palm, touching very lightly, like someone tracing a scar, then looked up at me with an earnest, I-don't-want-to-hurt-you expression that was as close as she got anymore to the look of longing I remembered. "Kenny, please—" she said. "Please don't do this."

I pulled my hand back, closed my eyes, and swallowed the salt at the back of my throat. Key West was a place we'd never been to, but I had an image of Dana on the beach in Evanston the summer before. It was one particular morning in August, just as the sun was coming up over the blue edge of Lake Michigan. We hadn't seen each other for a couple of months and we'd been up all night lying on a blanket in the park that ran along the lake. We'd made a vow to go swimming at dawn, as if it were necessary to memorialize the night with some kind of pagan ritual, and the image I had was of Dana rising up to me out of the cold water, shivering and naked, her hair streaming and her face shining with a promise that seemed to me unambiguous and absolute.

"We could go anywhere we wanted to," I said, opening my eyes and twisting the key in the ignition. The windshield wipers came on, tick-tocking back and forth, and I revved the engine a little to keep it from stalling. Everything seemed so simple: all we had to do was take off.

Dana was pulling off her gloves, finger by finger. Her hands were wonderfully gaunt and luminous, a fine point of bone at each wrist, and she held them in the warm current of air that came up from under the dash and rubbed them together as if she were rinsing them in water. "I can't, Kenny, I really can't. It's not just us. . . ." Her shoulders slumped. "I'm exhausted—that's the truth—there's not enough of me left over—"

I touched a curl at the back of her neck. "It's okay," I told her. "You wouldn't have to do anything—you could just lie in the sun, get some rest—" My arm was around her shoulders now, she was letting me pull her closer, and I could smell her hair—lemon and cigarette smoke and something else, something like feathers maybe, like the faint musk of eiderdown. When she began to stiffen, I said, "Did I ever tell you about my grandfather?"—thinking that if I went on talking maybe she wouldn't move. "The one whose car this was? He was my father's father. He died of a heart attack last week at the age of eighty-three."

My father and I had never gotten along, but I'd always been close to my grandfather. Back when I'd first gotten interested in reading, he would read the same books I did—the Hardy Boys and Albert Payson Terhune and then Edgar Rice Burroughs and C. S. Forester. The day before, at his funeral, I hadn't felt much of anything during the church service, but when we were standing beside the open grave after the coffin had actually been lowered into the ground, I suddenly found myself feeling nauseous and vaguely repelled. The grave was freshly excavated, and its sheared walls were cross-sectioned with veins of blue clay and networked with a tangle of tiny roots that were like exposed nerve endings. I had an image of my grandfather in his charcoal-gray suit lying down there inside of all that. I imagined him with his glasses on and his eyes wide open in the darkness. When it came my turn to scoop up a handful of clay to drop on the glossy lid of the coffin, I thought I was going to be sick. The feeling stayed with me until well afterwards, back at my aunt's house, when she took me aside and showed me the two lined sheets of legal-sized paper on which my grandfather had named and assigned each separate thing he valued. The sight of my own name on that list, penned in a precise, miniaturized longhand with india ink, had worked on me like an antidote and the nausea had subsided.

"Besides this car, he left me all his books, a silver fountain pen with a set of gold nibs, a breech-loading rifle from the Spanish-American War, all his rods and reels and fishing tackle, and this old bone-handled pocketknife." I reached into the deep pocket of my coat and pulled out the knife. Its handle was grooved like tree bark, smooth as yellowed ivory, the silver backs of the two closed blades arched slightly above the slot. "Here," I said, "take it."

Dana held out her hand and I gave her the knife.

"My grandfather was incredibly careful. He'd pay careful attention to whatever he was doing. Like this car, he'd rotate the tires according to a plan and keep the bearings greased and change the oil at the right time and do everything according to the season. Just the way he handled things made them seem special. I remember him paring apples for my grandmother with that knife—it was like each apple was a spool of ribbon he was unwinding. Go on," I said. "Open it up, see how easy it is to open."

"It's beautiful," Dana said in a small voice. She ran her finger over the worn handle. "What kind of bone?"

"I'm not sure," I said. "Probably elk, deer, something like that."

"It's so strange—" she said. "To think of it being alive once, running through the woods—" She pulled open the longer of the two blades and touched the ball of her thumb against the edge. "And now it's the handle of a knife I'm holding. . . ."

"Be careful," I said. "It's really sharp. You can cut hair with that thing. I could probably shave with it. Here, I'll show you. Close it first—" I reached out to help her but she was already folding the knife shut, and as the blade clicked back into place it slid into the web of flesh between the thumb and forefinger of my right hand. For a long moment it was as if nothing had happened, and then a dark bloom appeared against the pale glow of my skin—too black and sudden somehow to be blood, but spreading and running warmly down over my thumb.

Dana was fumbling with the knife, trying to get it open again. "Please," she said. "Please." But the blade was too slippery now, she couldn't get a grip. Instead of coming open, it closed more deeply, biting through some last obstruction of flesh and tearing loose. "Oh, God," Dana said. She let the knife drop and looked up at me, her eyes so wide the whites showed clear around the irises. "I must've cut an artery."

"It's okay," I said. I had my hands clasped together and was holding them out over the floor to keep from bleeding on the upholstery. My fingers were slick, and the throbbing numbness I felt had a dull edge to it that scared me. "Do you have any Kleenex? I'm getting blood all over everything."

Dana pulled a handful of tissues out of her purse and folded them into a thick wad to press against the cut.

"This sort of thing always looks worse than it is," I said.

She'd already taken another tissue and was wiping at my knuckles and the backs of my fingers with quick little pats and dabs. "Kenny, my God—you're going to need stitches—"

"No, it'll be all right. It's good that it's bleeding, it'll keep it clean." I heard the grinding sound of gears shifting and looked up, expecting to see the car parked in front of us, but it was no longer there. A dump truck spreading salt lumbered by, the loaded flatbed cantilevered so a thin stream of crystals sprinkled out past the loose flap of its tailgate.

The snow had finally stopped, leaving the air around the streetlights clear and black.

A few days after they'd determined she had cancer, Dana's mother had had her thumb amputated in an effort to keep the disease from spreading. When I'd met her the spring before, she had a trim, erect way of carrying herself that reminded me of Dana, but I couldn't remember what her hands looked like. Instead, I saw my grandfather's hands, freckled and covered with a light down of reddish-gold hair. The last time I'd seen him, he'd been painting a window frame on the side of the little clapboard house he'd moved into after my grandmother died. It was up in the mountains of central Pennsylvania, about fifty miles south of Harrisburg. Small, uninsulated, and without any heat to speak of, it had become the project to which he'd devoted the last five or six years of his life. For a moment now I could see the inquisitive and absorbed expression behind his wire-rimmed glasses as he brushed white paint on the windowsill with one hand and held a rulerlike metal shield against the edge of the glass with his other. On the dark rectangle of the windowpane itself fragments of green foliage, white cloud, and a piece of blue sky were reflected with a clarity that was almost photographic. As I pictured him like that, it occurred to me that if I left right away and drove all night I might be able to get to the cottage by morning. I remembered that he loved to sit on the porch sipping coffee and watch the morning light climb up the slopes of the westernmost mountains—and then it hit me that of course he wouldn't be there anymore. What I felt wasn't grief so much as a profound and surprised disequilibrium—the way you might feel if, coming suddenly upon your own reflection in a place you hadn't even known there was a mirror, you saw yourself not simply as someone else might see you, but for once, and only for a moment, as the absolute stranger you really were.

"I just thought of something," I said, and when Dana looked up at me expectantly, I felt myself go over some kind of hitch in the smooth seam of things.

"What is it?" she asked.

But I no longer knew—all that remained was a residue of feeling. "I'm not sure," I said. "Something about my grandfather. The last time I saw him he was painting a window frame on his house, and I was just remembering that now it's empty."

"How about your hand?"

"Fine," I said. "As far as I can tell." Tentatively relaxing the grip of my left hand, I found I could hold the wad of tissues in place with just my thumb. "I think I've stopped bleeding."

"It was like a nightmare—I could see the whole thing happening but I couldn't do anything, I couldn't even move—"

"It's all right now."

"But you can't possibly drive like that—and you've got to go to the infirmary right away—you'd better let me drive you—"

"I'm fine," I said. "Anyway, the shift's an automatic. All I need is one hand." To demonstrate how easy it was, I shifted into drive with my left hand and let the car roll forward a few feet. "Nothing to it," I said.

"You're sure? I mean it's almost twelve and Mrs. Brogan's at the desk, I've got to get back in. But I feel like it's all my fault. I want to do *some*thing—"

"It's nobody's fault—it just happened—"

"I know, I know, but God . . . I'm sorry—" She leaned forward and then sort of rocked back and forth. "Really, really sorry. . . ."

"It's okay, Dana. It'll be okay."

"No. You've got to go to the infirmary." She started buttoning her coat and pulling her gloves back on. "Right now. Otherwise . . . I don't know, but we can't have something else—" Her voice sounded desperate and a little dazed. "I just want you to go to the infirmary. Promise me you'll go right now. Promise—"

"Okay, I promise."

She brushed her lips against my cheek. "Oh, God, Kenny," she said. "I want you to be all right." She turned and pushed the door open. "Please, please, be careful."

A rush of cold air came into the car and for a second I felt like I was falling. Everything was going too fast. "Dana, listen—" I said, but I couldn't think of what to say. "I'll call you—"

She reached back to squeeze my arm. "Watch out for ice," she said.

Then she was out of the car. The door slammed shut behind her, and I watched as she made her way down the sidewalk, each step kicking up a little spume of snow. At the stone archway into her quad she looked back, raised her hand and waved once, then turned and disappeared.

I knew I couldn't face all those fluorescent lights at the infirmary, but I didn't want to go back to my room, either. All I could think of was to keep driving. At first, turning around and heading back out to the interstate, I thought I might actually drive to my grandfather's cottage in Pennsylvania—but then a couple of hours later, on the bypass east of Indianapolis, I began to see signs for Columbus, Ohio. Columbus was Dana's home town.

I wasn't sure exactly what I had in mind. Maybe I thought I'd be able to reach Dana through her mother—at least that would have made a certain kind of sense. But I don't remember thinking about Dana at all. The truth is, I wasn't thinking much about anything. Driving southeast from Chicago through the snow-covered flatness of Indiana, and then on into central Ohio, where the snow hadn't yet reached, my mind had been as clear as the night sky, which was like an inverted bowl, perfectly black and starless. I listened to the radio until the last stations signed off or faded into static, then I drove on in silence, glad to be driving, glad just to be going somewhere. The edge of my injured hand rested on the bottom rim of the steering wheel, my left hand curled around the top rim, and the wheel itself hardly even moved, the highway was so straight and deserted.

I'd never been to Dana's house before, but I knew the address and I was sure that when I got to Columbus I'd somehow be pulled magnetically to the right street. It took an hour of aimlessly driving around reading street signs before I finally gave up and got directions at an all-night gas station. The house I pulled up in front of was a semidetached brick colonial in a row of others exactly like it. There was a trimmed hedge under the first-floor windows, and I imagined that behind one of the windows on the second floor Dana's mother was in bed at that very moment, asleep and dreaming. Sitting there in the graying darkness, I felt a surge of anxiety at the enormous, hidden complexity of things— like looking out an airplane window at tiny automobiles on the streets below and realizing that inside each one of those moving dots were actual people with plans and feelings and things in their pockets.

When I woke up, the sun was shining in on my face through the windshield. My hand was throbbing and my neck was stiff, but according to my watch I hadn't been asleep very long. It was still early, only a few minutes past eight. I was sitting up staring at the curtained windows of the brick house, looking for some sign of activity, when the door opened and out came Dana's mother. She was wearing black slacks and a red sweater with the sleeves pushed up. Bending down to pick up the morning paper, she didn't look any different from what I remembered—if anything, she looked a little younger.

No sooner had the door closed behind her than I was out of the car and walking up the sidewalk. I had a giddy, floating sensation that events were converging in a way crucial to my life but beyond my actual control. Pushing the doorbell, I felt like I was delivering a telegram whose message I had no way of knowing.

The door swung open, and there was Dana's mother. "Yes?" she said through the glass door still closed between us.

I smiled as widely as I could manage. "You probably don't remember me," I said. "Kenny McAllister. I'm a friend of Dana's—we met last spring in Chicago."

"In Chicago," she repeated, and then, recognizing me, "Of course—Dana's young man." She frowned. "But what's the matter? Has anything happened?"

"No—everything's fine. I was just passing through—my grandfather died last week, and I was—I just thought I'd stop by and see how you were doing."

"Please." She pushed the storm door toward me and held it open. "I'm sorry, I'm afraid you took me a little by surprise. Come in, come in. Let me get you some coffee."

We walked through the living room and on into the kitchen. Everything I saw looked strange and familiar at the same time—a sofa with bright, flowery upholstery, a glass coffee table with an empty ceramic ashtray and several magazines arranged neatly in layers. On one of the end tables beside the couch was a framed photograph of Dana, her hair in a long, swept-back style I'd never seen before.

"You're probably on your way to work," I said. I knew she was the photography editor of some industrial or institutional magazine. "Don't let me hold you up. I really am just passing through—"

"Don't be silly," she said. She was standing at the kitchen counter with her back to me, and I watched as she reached up with both hands and took a cup and saucer from the cupboard. Without a thumb, her right hand looked vaguely like a talon, but all its movements had a streamlined, fluid sort of grace. "Where're you on your way to?"

The question confused me for a second, but then I remembered. "Pennsylvania. My grandfather has a cottage up in the mountains—or rather he had one. He died last week—a week ago last Friday—"

"Oh," she said, turning toward me. "I'm sorry—"

"His heart just evidently gave out. He was in his eighties. He lived by himself, so it was the mailman who actually found him—" I paused, vaguely embarrassed. "He gave me his car," I said to change the subject. "He left it to me. That's how I got here. It's an old Studebaker, but in really great condition."

"They're the ones that look so futuristic—" She finished pouring my coffee. "Cream and sugar?"

"No, black is fine."

"Your grandfather must be a lot on your mind."

"Not really, it's funny, not until last night—" I stopped again, then started to explain. "I cut myself with a pocketknife he left me—right there," I said, extending my hand as if I expected her to shake it.

"You'd better be careful it doesn't get infected," she said. She set the cup down. "I've got some Merthiolate in the bathroom—let this cool a minute, I'll be right back."

The newspaper was lying unfolded in front of me, and as I stirred the spoon in my coffee, I scanned the front page. SPACE PROGRAM UNDER FIRE, said one headline; AUTO WORKERS THREATEN STRIKE, said another. There was a picture of Johnson with someone I didn't recognize.

"I'm afraid this may sting a little." She was carrying a small reddish-orange bottle in one hand and cradling a box of Band-Aids against her chest with the other. She sat next to me and took my hand. Her fingers felt as smooth and dry as paper, and in profile her cheekbone stood out like a knob, stretching the skin and giving it a burnished, nearly translucent glow. Her hair was long and black, interwoven with wiry strands of silver and tied loosely at the back of her neck with a thin black ribbon. "You probably ought to get a tetanus shot," she said. "That's a deep cut." She unscrewed the bottle and used the little brush inside the cap to paint the pouch of skin between my thumb and forefinger a bright orange.

"Dana told me you were—" I didn't know how to say it. "—that you were sick," I finally managed. "And I just wanted to tell you how sorry I was, and see if there was anything I could, you know, if there was anything—"

"Yes, well," she said, coming to my rescue. "That's very kind." She finished peeling the paper from a Band-Aid and looked up at me. Her eyes were pale gray and the pupils were like tiny black seeds. "Actually, I'm doing better than anyone expected," she said. "Right now I'm in what they call remission—like a reprieve, except that it's usually only temporary." She smiled, then shrugged in a way that reminded me of Dana. "But it's funny—in spite of everything, I get the most overwhelming sense of gratitude sometimes—like a rush of adrenaline, the smallest things can set it off—" She stopped talking and looked down, then pressed the Band-Aid to my skin. "There," she said. "Not quite as good as new. Before you leave, remind me to give you directions to the hospital. You wouldn't want to come down with lockjaw." She snapped the lid of the tin box shut. "Can I get you some more coffee?"

"No, thanks," I said. "This is fine. I ought to be on my way." I carefully lifted the cup with my bandaged hand and took a long sip.

"How's Dana doing?"

I swallowed. "Dana's fine," I said. The coffee had a satisfying, bitter taste. Very gently, making sure not to let it rattle, I set the cup back down on the saucer. "To tell the truth, she broke up with me a few weeks ago. She says she doesn't want to give me any false hopes—"

"No?" Dana's mother laughed. "Sometimes I wonder if there're any other kind." She got up from the table and took the bottle of Merthiolate and the box of Band-Aids over to the counter. "But I guess, the way things are, you really can't blame her. Maybe she just needs time. Things change. That's one thing you can count on, isn't it?" She turned to the window over the sink. "Here we are still in March and look at those maple trees out there—they're already starting to bud."

"Some things don't change, though," I said. I didn't want any easy advice; I wanted to keep things straight. "Like my grandfather—he's gone for good."

"Yes," she said. "That's true. But everything alive changes—that's the difference, isn't it? Nothing's permanent until it dies."

"If you mean permanently absent—"

"Exactly. Always not there. Not there forever. Because that's a kind of presence, too. Like in the photograph of a face, except that it's in every moment that passes—" And as if to demonstrate, she raised her narrow hand and waved it horizontally through the air, in the motion of something floating down a fast current. "Do you see what I mean?"

"Yes," I said—and meant it: yes, everything that passed might leave behind an image of itself that lasted. The idea seemed so beautifully simple that for a long moment, as the clear light of it filled me, I felt on the verge of being healed.

A few minutes later, though, after Dana's mother had left for work and I was sliding back in behind the steering wheel of the Studebaker, I happened to glance down at the knife lying on the floor where Dana had dropped it, and somehow just the sight of the dried blood on its bone handle was enough to make me feel suddenly exhausted and more confused than ever. I picked it up and tried to wipe it clean with a little spit and a crumpled tissue, but the blood had gotten down into the handle's barklike texture of crevices and grooves and I was only able to clean it superficially. Putting it back in my pocket, I felt the breath go out of me and I lowered my head to the steering wheel. I remembered the time I'd watched my grandfather dress a squirrel with that same knife, how he'd split the belly open and shown me what was inside, giving me the heart to hold in my hand, unraveling the blue intestines. We'd salted the hide and tacked it to a board, then put it out in the sun because my grandfather said that would cure it. Remembering that made me laugh, and I raised my head from the wheel and turned the key in the ignition. I'd been thinking of continuing on to Pennsylvania or even of driving down to Key West by myself, but instead I turned around. I felt like I'd already used up wherever there was left to go. Dana's mother had given me directions to the nearest hospital, but I couldn't see much point in going there either. After all, if it were true that only what was lost really lasted, then fatality itself might be what saved me. That was the hope I held on to, anyhow, driving back through western Ohio and on into the vast, snow-banked fields of Indiana as the whole sunlit world slipped away behind me.

Ruth's Daughter

At the age of twelve—on the very day that she says she started bleeding for the first time—my mother was told by a gypsy fortune-teller to "beware of wheels." Nine years later, one particularly wet night in April, she and a young second lieutenant named Peter G. (for George) Hanson, the man destined to become my father, were on their honeymoon trip to Virginia Beach when he crashed the new car he was driving into the back of a stalled tractor-trailer, and my mother, who just previously had been sitting cozily beside him, smashed through the windshield and went flying out into the fog. She didn't almost die—she *did* die; her heart actually stopped beating. And then, after a black doctor named Reuben Benjamin started pounding on her chest while she still lay there in the road, it miraculously started up again.

My mother's name is Ruth. She has that same tenacity of spirit we associate with her namesake in the Old Testament, and when she tells you the part about her heart stopping, she'll slap the palm of her hand against her breast like someone trying to dislodge a fishbone from her throat. After the miraculous rescue, Ruth was sent to a hospital in New Rochelle, New York, where her nose was rebuilt from a piece of her own rib, her forehead and cheekbones were expertly reassembled, and her skin was sewn back together again so there was hardly any difference. Her face just took on the slightly asymmetrical cast that someone else's face has, someone familiar, when you happen to see it in a mirror.

A few months after Ruth was released from the hospital, my father got orders to Korea. He'd decided on a career in the Army while still in college, and he'd graduated from Lehigh the year before with a reserve commission, a degree in history, and a long, boyish face that people said made him look like Jimmy Stewart. By the time he left, Ruth was already pregnant with me, and by the time he got back I'd already started walking. Having me so quickly, I think, was simply Ruth's way of feeling whole again. She is a very purposeful woman; there is nothing in the least dreamy or lackadaisical about her. In fact, throughout my childhood I used to think she never really slept at all. She has a scar that crooks across her forehead like a finger. With makeup on it's hardly noticeable, but when she's sleeping it keeps one eyelid held slightly open. If the scar was one result of her accident, I was just as surely another. Ruth used to tell me she'd prayed for a daughter and gotten an angel instead, and I think my first stirrings must have felt to her like redemption. I know she had my name picked out from the very first, like something tucked away in a drawer just waiting for the right occasion: Rebecca Rachel—after her own mother and her mother's mother, both long since dead.

At the age of seventeen, just two weeks before my high school graduation, I discovered that I was pregnant myself—in my own case, quite unexpectedly. The growing certainty became absolute fact one dark and drizzly Friday morning in a fluorescent-lighted doctor's office in Aiken, South Carolina. My father had been transferred to Fort Gordon, which is in Georgia, and we'd been living in Augusta for about three years. By that time, we'd already lived all over the world, as I liked to say—Germany, Okinawa, Texas. I considered myself quite the world traveler. Compared to Dallas, where I'd gone to junior high, Augusta seemed like the very edge of nowhere; I couldn't wait for college to come along and carry me away. Augusta is also right on the Savannah River—all you have to do is cross over and you're in another state, which is exactly what I did as soon as I decided I had to see a doctor.

Things always seemed a little looser somehow in South Carolina, probably because you only had to be eighteen to buy beer over there. In my high school, crossing the river was associated with fake IDs and with generally doing things you weren't supposed to. In fact, I was parked over there, way back on a dead-end little two-rut trail in the woods, the night I'm sure the baby was conceived. The father was a sweet, romantic local boy named Robby Dodd Gleason. He had a cowlick at his forehead, and he wrote me poems as well as playing on the high school football team. We'd been going steady right through our senior year, but it was only the second time we'd actually gone all the way. We were parked in our special place over in the scrub pines across the river and Robby Dodd was touching me the way he always did, like he couldn't quite believe I was real. He'd start saying my name over and over again and I wouldn't be able to get enough of the way it sounded when he said it.

I liked Robby Dodd a lot, but I knew I wasn't in love. Or rather I thought, if this is love, then it isn't anything I can't handle. It was fun, but I expected to be in love a lot more times before I ever got married—*if* I ever got married, which was doubtful. I thought that great actresses (or great writers—I hadn't yet decided which I was) were better off not married. My mother had been brought back from the dead, literally resurrected, so that I might be born, and I assumed I'd probably just take a succession of lovers while I followed the rising star of my own unique fulfillment. But I was grateful to Robby Dodd. I didn't want to have to leave high school still a virgin, and I wanted to extend my emotional range as well. Most of all, I wanted to know that terrible, significant things were happening to me. Only by going through the fire, I believed, could my genius be tempered and made durable. As for being hurt, I'd decided I was exempt: Ruth had already paid my way.

When I left the doctor's office in Aiken, I was terrified, but somehow it was exhilarating too, like the charge of adrenalin you might feel as the curtain begins to rise on the great drama of your life. That afternoon when I got home from school, Ruth was doing something at the kitchen sink, coring an apple maybe or scrubbing the dirt off an Idaho potato. After raining all morning, the sun had unexpectedly come out in full force and it was pouring in through the window in front of her, spangling the tiny motes of dust in the air so that she seemed to be standing in a shower of miniaturized, nearly invisible confetti.

"Why's it so dusty in here?" I said.

"I don't think it's so much the dust this time of year as the pollen," Ruth said. She turned toward the window over the sink and pointed with an elbow. "Mostly from that locust and those two maples over there. It gets in the air and that's that, brother, there's not a thing you can do about it."

We looked out the window for a second, and then I said, "Why don't you sit yourself down and let me trim off your split ends? You've been looking a little frazzled around the edges lately. I'll even throw in a scalp massage, the whole deluxe treatment."

Ruth loved to have her hair worked on. She'd gone to beauty school and worked as a beautician for nearly two years before the accident. It must have been a perfect career for Ruth, ideally suited not only to her own physical vanity but also to her love of advising other people. Ruth herself has the kind of fine-textured yet naturally oily skin that never wrinkles, and her thick, abundant hair is the burnt-gold color of the sun in certain old Art Nouveau posters I've seen. I much prefer her intense, dramatic coloring to my own pallidness. I look more like my father: light-brown hair and eyes that are a sort of washed-out blue with little spikes of dark gray around the pupils. Ruth's eyes are as sea green as the eyes of a calico cat.

We stood at the kitchen sink while I washed Ruth's hair, and when I was through, she sat down at the kitchen table with a towel around her shoulders. I got behind her so I could comb out her hair.

"I don't know how to tell you this," I said.

"What?" She started to turn around to look at me, but I held her head.

"Just sit still and let me comb," I told her. I held the top of her head with one hand and tugged the metal teeth through her hair with the other, pulling carefully when I came to a snarl and spattering water each time I completed a stroke.

"I went to a doctor this morning over in Aiken—"

She started to turn her head again but I had a knot of hair caught in the comb and she couldn't turn very far. "Ow—that hurts," she said.

"Well, just hold still and wait a minute—"

"What do you mean you went to a doctor? What kind of a doctor? What's the matter?"

"An o-b-g-y-n," I said, spelling out the letters as if there were a child nearby who shouldn't hear what I was saying.

"Dear God in heaven—don't tell me."

She'd stopped trying to turn around now. She was sitting still. I tugged the comb through her hair and she tilted her head slightly forward against the tension of my pulling. I had expected my news to weaken her somehow—I think I even imagined her breaking into tears and reaching out blindly for something to hold on to. But nothing like that happened. Instead, she seemed, just sitting there, to take on weight, as if *she* were the one who was pregnant, not me.

"Well, we can't tell your father," she said. "At least not right away. I knew there was something—just as soon as you walked in the door, I knew it like a premonition. It was Robby Dodd, wasn't it?"

"Mother, Robby Dodd and I—"

"How far along are you?"

"About, I don't know, a little over two months, I guess. It's from a time I think back in April. We went to see *Dr. Zhivago.*"

"You went to see *Dr. Zhivago.*" Ruth shook her head back and forth. "Becky, Becky, Becky," she said. "Dear God in heaven, I can't believe it. We'll just have to figure out what to do, that's all." She sat still for a minute, as if she were listening to something; then she said, "I know what—I'll call Reuben Benjamin in Philadelphia, maybe he'll know the name of someone." Doctor Benjamin was in his seventies now; although he and Ruth had only seen each other a couple of times since the accident, they still exchanged Christmas cards every year.

"What do you mean the *name* of someone?"

"Don't worry," she said. "This thing doesn't have to ruin your life. Just let me think about it. It's not the end of the world, we'll figure something out." She ran her fingers through her damp hair. "Don't let me get too dry or you won't be able to see the split ends."

I went back to work and neither of us said anything for a while—there was just the whishing sound of the comb and then the clicking of the scissors, like someone going tut-tut-tut-tut. Gradually, some hold I'd had on myself all day began to let go, and pretty soon I was crying, the tears sliding quietly down my cheeks as I trimmed Ruth's hair. I wasn't ready to look her in the eyes yet, and I didn't want her to try to comfort me either, I felt too weak for that, so I tried to keep my breath from catching and just went on cutting. I didn't want to have a baby any more than Ruth wanted me to, and I was so relieved she'd taken over the whole problem of what to do I felt like I might float away. Now, I thought, I'll just be going along for the ride—Ruth will see to whatever has to be done, and I'll just be a sort of passenger.

By the time we made the trip to Philadelphia, it was the last day of June, nearly three weeks later. As far as my father knew, Ruth and I were just traveling around looking at colleges. Which in fact we were— what had begun as a deception turned into part of our mission and we must have visited half a dozen campuses by the time we got to Philadelphia. But if my father was pleased by our trip, Robby Dodd was thrown into despair. He didn't know about my being pregnant either (I still didn't show), but he believed that if I really loved him I'd be content to stay in Augusta and go to college there; otherwise, he said, our love was doomed. For my own part, I liked nothing better than the role of star-crossed lover, and I spent the early morning hours after our senior prom kissing the tears off Robby Dodd's face and promising that I'd go on loving him no matter what. A little while later, as we were crossing the Savannah River on our way back home, the sun came up, streaking the horizon an exquisite gold, and I reached out and traced my initials in the mist our breathing had made on the inside of the car window.

What happened was that the day after I told her, Ruth called Reuben Benjamin. He was long retired by then but, as predicted, he'd come through with the name of someone. Ruth had taken it down on a section of the perforated note paper she kept on a roll by the telephone, and as we were driving across the Ben Franklin Bridge into downtown Philadelphia she took it out of her bra and unfolded it for the third time that morning.

"Doctor Raymond Patterson," she said, offering up the syllables once again for our consideration. When I didn't respond, she glanced back at the creased paper in her hand and read the address. For some reason, we both found the sound of "Twenty-Two Eighty Greenwood Street" reassuring.

Ruth was driving and I was sitting next to her navigating. "When we get over the bridge just keep going straight," I said. "Then we turn south on Twenty-second."

"I've always thought I'd like to live in Philadelphia someday," Ruth said. "The City of Brotherly Love they call it—I never understood why that was—"

"William Penn was a Quaker," I explained. "Quakers are pacifists— like Gary Cooper in *Friendly Persuasion.*" That and *Gone with the Wind* were Ruth's all-time favorite movies.

"Isn't it funny I never knew that?" she said. "I just always thought it sounded so friendly." She glanced over at me. "How are you feeling? Why don't you have another soda cracker?" She felt around on the seat between us for the waxed-paper package of saltines she'd prescribed for my nausea.

"I'm fine, just watch where you're going," I said. "God, look at this place. I can't believe how run-down everything looks."

"A lot of very wealthy people live in Philadelphia," Ruth told me. "Didn't you ever hear of the Main Line? Grace Kelly's family is from Philadelphia."

"I think we're headed for a slightly different neighborhood," I said.

The farther into the city we drove the more depressed I was getting. Everything looked dirty and dilapidated. Rows of adjoining houses faced flush on the street with nothing but a raised step or two between the door and the sidewalk. All the streets seemed to be named after trees, but what few trees there were looked scrawny and wilted. It was only a little after ten in the morning, but the humidity was already at work like an extra force of gravity, compressing the heat until it actually seemed to liquify over the hoods of the cars parked along Greenwood Street. A few people were out walking, but there wasn't another white face in sight.

"There it is," Ruth said. "That must be it there where the shingle is. Twenty-Two Eighty."

"What time is it? We still have to park," I said.

"Don't worry, we've got plenty of time. Do you feel okay?"

"I just want this to be over with," I said.

"Pretend you're someone else," Ruth said. "That's what I do. When it's something bad, I just pretend it's happening to someone else. I put myself into a kind of trance. Nothing can touch you if you don't let it. If you have to, Becky, you can turn yourself into steel."

"I'm trying," I said. "I just hope it doesn't hurt—"

"At some point *everything* hurts," Ruth said.

"Gee, thanks. That cheers me right up," I said. And in fact it did: it felt like the truth, and the worse it was the more satisfaction there was somehow in facing it.

"There is nothing free in this life," Ruth told me. Then she said, "I think I see a space." She pulled a quick U-turn at the next intersection, drove back a block and parked in front of a laundromat with a boarded-up window and the front door propped open. A young black woman was standing in the doorway smoking a cigarette. Next to her was a sign that said COIN-O-MATIC and behind her were the revolving blades of an electric ceiling fan. I could feel the woman's eyes on us while we rolled up the windows and locked the car. When we got out, I was afraid Ruth might say something loud enough for her to hear. All I wanted was to be invisible. I remembered Ruth's trick: this isn't really me, I thought, this isn't really me. I kept my eyes on the ground and simply followed my mother. I was wearing sandals and I watched the delicate way the thongs crisscrossed over my insteps. Watching my feet made me feel detached. I admired the high curve of the arches, the round little toes. They really might have belonged to someone else.

We turned in at a house with entrance stairs and a narrow porch. There was a brass nameplate, but before I could read it the door swung open and out stepped a white man in a blue uniform. He wore a peaked cap with a badge. It was only the mailman, but in the instant before I saw his leather pouch, I thought it was the police, and the full cup of my steady low-grade nausea suddenly started to tip.

"Oh," I said. I turned to one side, leaned over, and let it spill. Ruth handed me a Kleenex and I stood there wiping at my mouth, keeping still while I waited for the nausea to pass.

"Are you ladies all right?" the mailman asked. "Do you need a hand?"

"Isn't that kind of you," Ruth said. "I'm sure we'll be fine. We're just on our way to see the doctor."

"She'll feel better out of the sun," the mailman said. As he went past us, his fat pouch brushed against my bare arm.

"Let's just get inside, please," I said to Ruth. "I've got to sit down."

She pushed open the door for me and we walked out of the bright light into semidarkness. A fan was humming. A slight breeze from it lifted the hair away from my neck.

"Why don't you sit right down," Ruth said. "I'll let the nurse know we're here. I think we're a few minutes early." Her voice was loud in the room's quiet dimness.

Ruth walked over to the reception window, and I sank into an easy chair with crocheted doilies on the arms. There were some other people in the room, but I didn't want to look at them. On the table beside me, next to a lamp with an ornamental base and a fringed shade, was a pile of magazines. I pulled an old *Life* off the top and started leafing through it. Except for the sliding glass panels in the opposite wall, the room wasn't anything like a doctor's office. It reminded me of my father's aunt's house in Wilmington, Delaware. The shades were drawn against the heat, so the light had an antique, submerged quality, like a sepia photograph. In off-hours this was obviously somebody's living room. An old upright piano with stacks of sheet music piled across the top stood against the wall next to the electric fan. The room smelled not of antiseptic but of cooking and pipe smoke and old paper. It was a musty, comforting smell.

"My daughter has an appointment," I heard Ruth say. "But I guess we're probably a little early—"

"Name?"

Across from me, sitting on a scroll-armed sofa with three scalloped doilies fastened to its back, was a pretty young black woman and a little boy of about three or four. She was fanning herself with a *National Geographic* and he was playing a game—sliding slowly off the sofa and then boosting himself back up, sliding slowly off again. When I raised my eyes to watch, he gave me a big delighted grin. He was crouched on the floor, having just completed a descent.

"Jesse, stop that and sit still," the woman said. "Get back up here." She slapped the cushion beside her.

A dapper little man with a mustache was sitting in the armchair next to the piano. He had on a suit and tie, but he looked perfectly cool nonetheless. "Is your name Jesse?" he said to the boy. "What do you know about that? My name's James. Maybe you and me ought to team up." He cocked his finger at the boy and laughed. The woman didn't even give him a glance.

"Rebecca Hanson," I heard Ruth say. "I'm her mother. Doctor Benjamin referred us. I made the appointment myself not three weeks ago. It must be there."

Every time I turned a page of the *Life* magazine, the breeze from the fan would make it quiver slightly in my fingers. I tried to ignore the conversation at the reception window by focusing on an advertisement for a kidney-shaped swimming pool with turquoise-colored water. Esther Williams was smiling at me from the pool's blue-and-white tiled edge. She had evidently just surfaced after making one of her perfect dives. Water was still clinging in droplets to her bathing cap.

"We'll just wait until he can spare us a minute then," I heard Ruth say. When I looked up again, she was taking a seat next to the pretty black woman on the sofa. She looked at me and shrugged. I nodded and immediately went back to my magazine before she could try to explain anything in front of these other people. A few minutes passed without anyone speaking, then the nurse came out of her office and said, "Mrs. Hanson, will you and your daughter step this way please?"

We followed her down the hallway to a small room where a heavyset black man was sitting behind a desk. He stood up, shook our hands, and waved at a couple of chairs. "Mrs. Hanson, Miss Hanson," he said. "Please sit down. I'm sorry, but there seems to be some misunderstanding. You say you talked with me on the telephone, but I have no recollection of such a call." His voice was a rich baritone, like an actor's, and there was a slight Caribbean lilt to it.

Ruth sat forward in her chair and while she repeated my story I could imagine the look on her face—eyes narrowed, her mouth tightened, the barely visible groove of a scar shining through the makeup over her left eyebrow. When she finished, the doctor sat back in his chair and clasped his hands in front of him. He was wearing a brown vest and a green bow tie. Nodding his head, he looked speculatively at my mother; then he turned his eyes on me. I was staring at the back of a double picture frame that stood on his desk. Probably photographs of his wife and children, maybe pictures of Barbados or Guadeloupe. I felt not only inadequate to my role but completely subsumed by it—as if, before, I'd been opaque, and now I'd become as transparent as a piece of glass. I realized it wasn't invisibility I wanted after all—it was just the reverse.

When I didn't meet his eyes, the doctor turned back and faced my mother. His hair was cut very close to his head and the thin line of a part had been shaved high on one side. "Excuse me, but I think I see the problem," he said. "I am not Doctor Patterson. I am Doctor Bonnard. Doctor Patterson's office is across the street. You have come to the wrong doctor."

"But I told the nurse Doctor Patterson," my mother said. "I'm sure I did. If this is some kind of joke, it better not be, because it's not very funny—"

Dr. Bonnard sat with his elbows on the armrests of his swivel chair, his hands still clasped in front of him like a child playing This Is the Church, This Is the Steeple. He opened his fingers. "I am afraid there is no joke here," he said.

The right doctor turned out to be at Twenty-Two Eighty-*Three* Greenwood Street. We left Dr. Bonnard's office like two people who have come to the party on the wrong night. We walked back through the breezy semidarkness of the waiting room and out once more into the oppressive glare of the street. I knew we'd be late now for sure. I didn't wear a watch, but according to Ruth's it was almost eleven o'clock. Of course, Ruth's watch was only ever approximate—she always set it fast or slow on purpose and then could never remember which or by exactly how much.

I was furious. "I can't believe this is actually happening," I hissed when we were out on the sidewalk. "This is absolutely unbelievable. How could you take me to the wrong doctor? How can that happen? I'm *relying* on you, Mother, you're supposed to be *helping* me—"

Before I could say anything else, Ruth grabbed the upper part of my arm and shook it once. She looked at me hard and said, "I am doing the best I can. I am sorry if what happened back there embarrassed you, but that is the least of it. Do you understand? That is nothing. There are more important things to think about right now. Those people don't know anything about us—or us about them. Let it go, Becky, forget about it, it just doesn't matter." She let go of my arm and brushed some loose hair away from my eyes.

I didn't apologize, but she'd made me feel better. I wanted her to be right, I wanted it not to matter, so finally I took her hand and we walked across to Twenty-Two Eighty-Three, which also had a nameplate on the door. R. PATTERSON, M.D., it said, and underneath, OBSTETRICS AND GYNECOLOGY. Since this place also looked more like somebody's home than a doctor's office, Ruth rapped on the door and we waited a minute to see if anyone would answer. The top half of the door was made of glass—set in square little panes, I remember, like in the snow-drifted windows on Christmas cards—but there was a pleated lace curtain behind it and you couldn't see in. Ruth was about to turn the knob when the door suddenly swung open, and we found ourselves facing a little old black woman who was so hunched over and wizened she hardly looked real—she was like someone in a fairy tale. She had a wooden cane that looked like a gnarled root and, despite the heat, a shawl over her shoulders and a kerchief around her head.

"We're here to see Doctor Patterson," my mother said.

The old woman didn't say a word. Instead, she turned away from the door and motioned with her cane for us to follow. We entered a hallway with a staircase at the end and, to one side, a parlor that might have been a replica of the waiting room we'd just left. The shades were drawn here too, but in the filtered, brownish light, I had an impression of old armchairs and hassocks, framed photographs on a table, a curved sofa with antimacassars on the back. I half expected to see another little Jesse grinning up at me from the floor. The old woman stepped into the room's arched doorway and pulled on a tasseled cord that hung down by the jamb. Up on the wall above her was a little brass bell. She rang it three times; then she turned back to us, stamped her cane on the floor, and pointed with it toward the staircase at the end of the hall.

"Thank you," my mother said. "Thank you very much."

The old woman made no sign of having heard. She was hobbling back into the parlor. A lamp with an orange shade was turned on next to a rocking chair, and on the table a Bible lay open under a large round magnifying glass. The pages were all tipped with red, and the soft black covers were crimped up around the book's edges.

We'd just started toward the stairs when we heard footsteps coming down. The first we saw of Dr. Patterson was his shoes—they were shiny black bedroom slippers, pointed at the toe—followed by black trousers and a patterned green tunic with three-quarter sleeves. When his face came into view, it had a wide smile and his teeth shone white inside the dark circle of his mustache and goatee. His hair was cut in a modified Afro (the first I'd ever seen), and it gave him a disconcerting electrified look. He exuded the confident energy of a very handsome man—it was like a magnetic tug that made you immediately pull back and go on the alert.

"Mrs. Hanson?" he said. "It had better be you because I didn't make any other appointments today. And you must be Rebecca. Reuben sends his regards. I'm Ray Patterson. Come on up, I keep my office right upstairs here. I'm afraid you may have had some trouble finding me." He talked rapidly and unselfconsciously, without any of the usual nervous formality of people meeting for the first time.

"I'm sorry we're late," my mother said. "But somehow we got the wrong address and ended up at the doctor across the street. He just sat there and let me tell him everything—I hope it won't make any trouble—"

"Doctor Bonnard? That sanctimonious old faker? Believe me, you didn't tell him anything he doesn't already know, one way or another." He ushered us into a small room that looked like the study in a Sherlock Holmes movie. There were glass-fronted bookcases, a wing chair behind a Victorian desk, worn oriental rugs, and burgundy-colored drapes. It was much cooler in here. I could hear the hum of an air-conditioner and smell the eucalyptus scent of what I thought was room deodorant until I noticed some kind of stick smoking in a thin vase and realized it must be incense.

"Brother Bonnard is not only a doctor, he is also a self-appointed minister of the Lord. But Brother Bonnard's own medical conduct is not exactly what you would call beyond reproach. I guess you could say he writes a few more prescriptions than he absolutely should. Other things too, things he might prefer his congregation didn't know and which it happens I *do* know. So he and I are still at deuce. Plus which, he ain't 'bout to go messin' with no white folks, you dig—" Dr. Patterson leaned back and laughed. He was sitting on a corner of the desk with one of his slippered feet dangling, and when he laughed he opened his mouth and tilted his head back so that from where I was sitting I had a strange glimpse of his throat and the gold fillings in his upper teeth.

I looked over at Ruth and saw that she was pretending to laugh along with him. With a shock I realized that from this point on she didn't know any more about what to expect than I did.

Almost as if he'd been reading my mind, Dr. Patterson looked at each of us in turn and said, "Just so you don't feel any more up in the air about what's going on than you have to, let me explain exactly what I'm going to do. At this stage of pregnancy, the fetus is too developed for suctioning and scraping." He looked at me and smiled as if this were very good news indeed. "There'll be no need for any scraping at all. Instead, we will simply induce a miscarriage, and the body will expel the fetus *naturally*. But before that occurs, you have got to be properly dilated, and that means a dilator and an iodine pack—just wads of cotton gauze, not much worse than a tampon—except for a little cramping you'll hardly feel a thing. The packing will stay in overnight, and then tomorrow morning I'll do the injection. After that you'll go through a kind of false labor to expel the fetus. We could do the whole thing here, but I'd prefer not to because it will take some time. Instead, I've made arrangements with a very reliable woman who is also a trained practical nurse. You'll stay at her house tonight; then tomorrow morning I'll come by and give you the injection. It won't be possible for me to be present throughout the expulsion process itself, but she will. Her name is Evangeline Williams. She works the night shift at Holy Redeemer, so she's at home right now, and she's expecting both of you. I'll give you directions and you can drive over there just as soon as we're finished here. I believe we've already discussed the financial arrangements. As a sign of good faith, I'll take half the money now, in cash, and then you can give me the balance tomorrow morning when I perform the injection. How does that sound?" His eyes came to rest on my mother.

Ruth had been nodding her head as he talked, and now she looked over at me. "Does that sound all right to you?"

"I didn't realize we'd have to stay overnight," I said. "Why can't we just go to a motel and come back in the morning?"

"You could probably do that, of course," Dr. Patterson said. "But I'd prefer you to be with some qualified person like Mrs. Williams. In any case, you can't stay here after the injection, and at that point it may be difficult, you know, to travel. I'd like you to be someplace where you won't have to move. I think we're very fortunate that Mrs. Williams is available. Frankly, I'm not at all sure I'd have decided to help you otherwise—"

So that was that. We agreed all around, and then Ruth opened her pocketbook. She took some bills from an envelope and counted out five of them, placing each one on the desk in front of Dr. Patterson as if she were dealing out a poker hand. He shuffled them into a neat stack and folded it exactly in half before slipping it into his pocket. Then he turned to me and smiled and again I felt all the force of his attention. It made me feel clumsy and shy, like being on the first date you really care about. I wanted very much for him to take charge of things, but I also resented his power—it was in such contrast to my own awkwardness and dependence. It diminished me, and there was a part of me that hated him for it. But even that part felt pleasantly stirred, as if a secret pulse, normally at rest, had suddenly started to beat.

Before getting down to business, he gave Ruth a copy of the morning paper and told her to make herself at home. Then he took me into another room so he could examine me and put in the iodine pack. The examination and the rest of it seemed unreal: sitting with my breasts exposed while a strange black man with electrified hair listened to my heart through a stethoscope, lying on the table under a white drape with my legs pulled back and my feet in the metal stirrups while his fingers pumped up the nausea inside of me like a balloon.

"I'm going to be sick," I said, trying to sit up and lean over.

"That's cool," he said. "Just do whatever you have to."

I retched but nothing came up and then the wave passed.

"How much more?" I asked.

"Almost done. Just lean back and count to ten real slow."

I did it, closed my eyes and counted, and a long time seemed to go by. It felt like the lower part of my body was a lump of clay, and I was counting the strokes it would take to mold the clay into my own natural shape. Then, after a while, I opened my eyes and Dr. Patterson's back was to me. He was taking off his rubber gloves, running water in the sink—talking to me, but I was missing what he said. The running water made it hard to hear. There was something else too—a humming sound, like someone singing. I thought it was coming from me for a second until I realized it was only the air-conditioner in the window.

By the time we finally found Evangeline Williams's house, it was late afternoon. We'd gotten lost twice by then and also stopped for lunch at one of those railroad-car diners with chrome stools at a counter. I felt like I was carrying a pillow between my legs, but I'd regained my appetite soon after leaving Dr. Patterson's office, and I remember I ate a tuna-melt on toast and, defiantly, a bowl of tomato soup—more than I'd eaten at one sitting in a couple of days. It really felt in some ways like we'd gotten through the worst, and I guess I was hungry with relief. But by the time we reached our destination, I was more closed-down and irritable than ever. Sweat was rolling down my sides and I was wondering if I might not have a fever. At one point, while I was holding the back of my hand against my forehead to see if it felt hot, I realized I must look exactly like the besieged heroine in some old-fashioned melodrama, but it didn't even make me smile.

The address we were looking for was on a narrow street lined with parked cars, one of them up on blocks with the rusted wheel drums showing. Three boys wearing knit caps but no shirts were walking down the sidewalk. I heard one of them say, "I ain't lyin', Jack, that mutha blew-*e-e-e!*—I mean *sky*-high!" and they all laughed. The house we wanted had a small front yard with a chain-link fence, and Ruth opened the gate and latched it behind us as gingerly as if she'd come to sell something. When she rang the doorbell, I said, "Avon calling," but before Ruth could say anything back, a little girl opened the door. "Why, hello, there," Ruth said. "Is this the Williams residence?"

The girl must have been about four or five. Her hair was tied in braids with little yellow and red ribbons all over her head, and she was wearing a loose, sleeveless dress. She had a round face with great, vivid eyes.

"Yes, ma'am," she said. Then she turned and called, "Mama, it's the ladies." She stood aside for us to come in, gestured toward the living room, and with a perfectly deadpan expression said, "Mama say if I be good I can have ʳparklers for the Fourth of July. You can watch me if you want to."

"That sounds real nice," I said. "I'd like that."

"My name is Sarah Williams," she said. "Pretty soon I be old enough to ride on the school bus. My birthday is August the third." Saying this she suddenly seemed to go shy. She turned to one side and started pulling at a loose thread at the hem of her dress.

There was a window fan in the living room, but it didn't seem to do much good—it was perceptibly hotter in here than outside. What with the heat and everything else, I felt like I might faint—that's what I'd do if I were a real Southern belle, I remember thinking—but instead I tried to brace myself against the back of a chair. I didn't want to chance sitting down until I'd been to the bathroom.

"Sarah, look at you standing there like a bump on a log," someone said in a soft, fluty voice—not scolding but not teasing either. "Can't you tell our guests to have a seat?"

I turned to see a tall, very dark-skinned woman coming down the carpeted stairs. She was wearing a long, flowing caftan and she had her hair in a turban knotted at the back. Her eyes were wide-set and tilted, and her posture as she came down the stairs seemed almost absurdly erect—like a soldier, I thought, or like a child playing grown-up.

"I'm Evangeline Williams," she said. "You all must be weary to the bone. Please sit down. I'm afraid you've caught us in the middle of one of our Philadelphia heat waves. Can I fix you a glass of iced tea?"

"Oh, yes," I said. "Please. But first can I use your bathroom?"

"Top of the stairs," she said. "Can you manage all right?"

"I think so."

"Good. If you have a dizzy spell or need to lie down all of a sudden, your room's right across the hall."

"Thanks," I said. "I do feel a little peculiar."

At that point apparently I went as white as a sheet and then, like a piece of laundry sliding off a clothesline, I just sort of folded down onto the floor.

When I opened my eyes it was almost dark. I was stretched out on a sofa, and for a certain period of time I lay there without knowing exactly where I was or why. It was a pleasant, floating sensation and I didn't want to lose it. I seemed to be completely alone. The only noise was the soft whirring of a fan. I lay very still and watched the way everything white in the room gradually sponged up all the light, until finally the air grew mottled with darkness and there was less light in a window than in the back of a butterfly chair. I closed my eyes, and when I opened them again a lamp was turned on and I was looking up into the shining eyes of the little black girl with ribbons in her hair.

"Hello, Sarah," I said. "I guess I've been asleep. What time is it?"

She dropped her eyes and shrugged.

"Where is everybody?"

She raised her eyes back to mine. She was a very solemn, no-nonsense sort of little girl who seemed to be aware of carrying some grave responsibility. When she pointed upstairs, I was reminded of the ancient woman who'd answered Dr. Patterson's door.

"Cat got your tongue?" I teased.

She stuck it out so I could see for myself, not as a joke but as a simple demonstration of fact. Then she put a finger to her lips and I understood that Ruth must be upstairs taking a nap.

"Did your mother already go to work?" I whispered.

Sarah nodded her head and whispered back, "Mama say when you all wake up we can have some pea soup."

"Are you awful hungry?"

She dropped her eyes, put her hands behind her back, and started twisting from side to side so her dress swirled back and forth at her knees.

Sitting up I discovered that I felt much better. For the time being anyway, there was no nausea. Also, the fever seemed to have left me cool and strangely clear-sighted. Everything I looked at, whether close-up or far away, had the same sharp-edged definition—like the clarity of objects in a surrealist painting or the exaggerated focus of certain photographs. I could see the crosshatching in a window screen across the room, each interstice geometrically precise, and the tiny coils of hair at Sarah's temples were each as contoured and three-dimensional as a shiny piece of wire.

"Don't worry, we'll eat in just a minute," I told Sarah. Then I got off the sofa and went upstairs to look for Ruth.

I found her in a bedroom at the top of the stairs. In the wedge of light from the hall, I could see her lying on her back in her half-slip and brassiere. With her arms outstretched and her legs parted, she looked like a long-distance swimmer taking a break. I could see the white of her eye in a little crescent where the left eyelid failed to go all the way closed. Her dress was folded neatly at the foot of the bed, and she was lightly snoring. I was thinking I hated to wake her up when the doorbell suddenly started ringing and her eyes snapped all the way open. She looked at me vaguely for a second and then, when the doorbell rang again, seemed to realize all at once that it wasn't me who'd wakened her.

"I wonder who that is," I said.

"Wait." She stood up, pulled on her dress and turned around for me to zip her up. "You wait here," she said. "Let me handle this. Mrs. Williams said not to let anyone in—especially not Doctor Patterson. She said not to worry a bit—he's a fine doctor, one of the best. But you know how these people are. She said he likes to gamble sometimes and if he's been drinking and losing he might come looking for the other half of his money—"

"Oh, God," I said. I sat down on the edge of the bed. It had a white chenille coverlet. From this angle the hall light was in my eyes and I felt like I might be sick again. "I'm going to wait in the bathroom," I said. "This kind of stuff really makes me nauseous—I just have to forget it's happening."

"Nothing *is* going to happen, Becky. Just keep your mind on that."

Ruth started down the stairs and I went across the hall into the bathroom. I closed the door and turned on the water so I wouldn't have to hear anything else. Then I held my hair back with one hand and leaned over the toilet. I stared down at the little pool of water in the bowl and waited to see if I was going to be sick. Water was splashing in the sink, a fine spray occasionally tickling the side of my face, and I stood there and thought of the absolute strangeness—in all the infinity of time and space—of my being right in that precise spot at that particular moment. There was a rust stain at the bottom of the toilet bowl, down where it tunneled into the plumbing, and I remember thinking: now this stain will be something I'll remember, carry with me wherever I go, forever. I was here because I'd been with Robby Dodd Gleason in the backseat of his father's car, but the simple connection between that moment and this one seemed unfathomable, as if the floor had just dropped out from under me. It wasn't so much something I thought as something I felt, a physical sensation, like light or sound—which isn't to say that I felt suddenly enlightened or informed, because I didn't. Just the opposite: I felt a sense of unknowing that was like some kind of vertigo. It made me reach down and hang on to the cool enamel edge of the bowl.

And then it all came up—everything I'd eaten at the diner so defiantly. Afterwards, I leaned over the sink and washed my face, rinsing my mouth until the acid taste was gone. I stood up and was looking at myself in the mirror when I heard Ruth outside the door.

"Becky? Are you all right? Let me in, I'll hold your forehead for you." She rattled the doorknob.

"It's open," I said.

That's me, I was thinking, looking in the mirror. But the idea seemed preposterous, like a plan to build a bridge across the ocean. What impressed me about the person in the mirror was that she was perfectly opaque. I knew I was supposed to be somewhere behind that surface, but the idea was impossible. To prove it, I reached out and pulled the mirror open. I looked into the medicine cabinet at shelves of plastic vials with typed prescription labels, an aspirin bottle with a red cap next to a blue jar of Noxema, adhesive tape on a metal spool and two rolls of cotton gauze, shiny eyebrow tweezers, manicure scissors and a man's shaving brush, its bristles shading from wheat-color down to jet black.

"The door's locked, it won't open," Ruth said, still rattling the knob.

I reached over and flushed the toilet. "Sorry—I didn't realize it was locked." I turned the button on the knob from vertical to horizontal and opened the door.

"Here I am," I said. "Everything's all right."

"Thank goodness. I thought you might be having some kind of reaction or something—"

"No," I said. "Nothing like that. Just the usual."

"Listen to this, Becky, you'll never believe it. That was none other than Doctor Patterson, but he wasn't drunk—he was every inch the gentleman. He just came by to check in on us and—Becky, I honestly think he wanted me to go out on the town with him—you know, like on a date. I didn't know whether to laugh or cry. Can you imagine?"

Without really feeling anything, I discovered that tears were streaming down my cheeks, and then I was sobbing.

"Becky?" Ruth said. "What is it, honey? What's the matter?"

All I could do was shake my head. I didn't know what the matter was, I didn't know anything at all. I turned away from Ruth and started to reach across the sink for a Kleenex to wipe my eyes, but then I realized I'd have to go in front of the mirror again so I used the backs of my fingers instead.

Ruth put her arms around me and tucked my head into her shoulder. "There, there," she said, patting my back and rocking me gently, "there, there."

Dr. Patterson came back at about ten-thirty the next morning. He showed up wearing cutoff jeans and a navy blue T-shirt that said CHUCKY'S RIBS in white block letters. It was the Fourth of July and he was on his way to a softball game and picnic. "I wish y'all could come too," he said, smiling at my mother. "Eat some hot barbecue, drink some cold beer—then, later on, after dat ol' evenin' sun go down, just lay back on a blanket and, you know, let the fireworks begin. Should be quite a show—I bet we might even run into the good Reverend Bonnard himself kickin' up his heels—"

Ruth looked over at me—we were having coffee with Mrs. Williams in the kitchen—and said, "I'm afraid that's not exactly the sort of day we had planned—nice as it does sound."

Mrs. Williams snorted and shook her head. "Raymond Patterson, you just better do what you came for, and then go on and leave us alone to take care of ourselves."

"Yes, ma'am! Yes, ma'am!" he said. "Maybe I'll come back and check you out later."

"The hell you will." Mrs. Williams stood up and started collecting our cups and saucers.

"Where's Sarah then? I bet she'd like to go."

"She's outside watching some other fools play with fire. We told her she better not mess with that trash unless she wants to get herself burned." She turned on the faucet and started rinsing out the cups.

"Well, Mama knows best—that's what I always say, don't I, Mama?" He laughed.

"Raymond, you just better quit," she said. "Now just go on and do what you have to do. This girl wants all this mess over with—don't you, Rebecca?"

"The sooner the better," I said, trying to look cheerful.

Ruth was wearing the slightly glassy-eyed and expectant half-smile she gets when she isn't sure what she's supposed to say. There was a flirtatious tension in the air that was unmistakable and yet—given our circumstances, et cetera—totally unthinkable. I was actually blushing when Dr. Patterson followed me upstairs to give me the injection. I lay back on the bed, opened my legs, and closed my eyes like a Victorian virgin on her wedding night. Then he started pulling out the packing, and I had an image of myself unraveling.

"Oh, yes, the cervix has dilated very nicely," he said. "Now, all it takes is a little salt water . . . you won't even feel this go in—there, that's it . . . that's it . . . and now it's all over, you can relax . . . don't get up though, just stay right there and in a little while you'll feel the contractions begin—maybe sooner, maybe later. Once they start, Evangeline will tell you what to do. Just relax and let the contractions do their work. Then, when she tells you, bear down like you're going to the bathroom—the fetus is still small so it should be relatively easy."

"Compared to what?" I asked. His cool, confident tone was beginning to make me angry.

"Compared to actually giving birth," he said.

But it *was* like giving birth. I was in labor all afternoon, while Dr. Patterson was out playing softball and eating barbecue. I hung on to Ruth and to Evangeline and I strained and sweated and felt something rupture deep down inside of me, rupture irreparably, and still it wouldn't come out, one great globe of pain just seemed to open up onto another, like an endless series of concentric Chinese boxes, each one egg-shaped and utterly impervious.

Evangeline had put a rubber mat under the sheets, and I lay in puddles of my own water and blood, soaking in sweat and groaning so steadily it turned into a chant. After a while, Evangeline took it up with me and pretty soon we had our own work song. "Push, now baby, push—" she'd say. "Uhh, that's right, now, uhh—"

Ruth kept the washcloth cool against my forehead, and she was crooning along with us. The odd thing was, we all seemed to be singing. The windows were open too, and outside I could hear firecrackers going off and kids yelling and laughing, but over everything else there was the sound of the three of us chanting and crooning to one another.

"Almost over," Ruth kept saying, "almost over," and, "That's right, Becky, that's right," and then Evangeline said, "There it is, I've got it!" and I felt myself give way, as if a door I'd been straining against had suddenly burst open and sent me sailing headlong out into the unresisting air.

We couldn't see each other's faces in the dark; we could only hear each other's voices. Evangeline and Sarah; Ruth and me: we were sitting out in the small bricked-in yard behind Evangeline's house. They'd brought me outside because of the heat, and I was stretched out on a chaise longue looking up at the crescent of light shining from under the moon's lowered lid. What kept coming back to me was an impression of something slippery and coiled sliding into a metal pan and Ruth, thunderstruck, whispering before she could think not to: "A girl, it's a little girl—"

After it was over, they'd sponged me clean and changed the sheets on the bed and while my body settled back into place, still quaking with little interior tremors that were like the echoes of my contractions, I'd gone in and out of sleep. Sleep would come and go, and my tears would come and go, and after a while sleeping and waking, crying and not crying, came to feel so much alike it was hard to tell the difference, as if each had met the other in some washed-out neutral place.

So time had passed and evening had come on and imperceptibly it had grown darker. Evangeline had brought me a cool, sweet soup and Ruth had held my hand while Sarah sang me a song about a journey. Now we were sitting outside in the dark. The tide had ebbed, you might say, and left us beached there on the shore, glad to be out of it, feeling as scoured as driftwood is by the currents we'd passed through. It was cooler out there and we thought we might be able to see the fireworks—but our angle of vision must have been wrong, all we could do was hear them. Somewhere on the other side of us, there'd be a string of small, popping explosions and then a great, ear-shattering BO-O-OM!, followed by the collective "Ah-h-h" of all the people who could see.

"That's all right, Sarah, never you mind," Evangeline said. "We don't need their old fireworks—we'll put on a show of our own."

"Yaay!" Sarah shouted. "Sparklers!"

"Just hold it steady now, baby, and I'll light it for you. Keep it away from your face now, don't get burned—"

The sparkler fizzed into life, shooting out tiny spokes of light all around Sarah's outstretched fist. She lifted it up high, as if it were a wand or a torch, and we were all caught by the sparkler's incandescent sizzling. Then, gradually, the fiery white bead at its core dropped to a point just a few inches above Sarah's hand and went out. All that was left was a bright ember.

"Isn't that pretty!" said Ruth. "Just like a falling star!"

Sarah looked at it for a moment and then started whipping the burned-out stick through the air, streaking its red glow into ellipses and perfect circles of light, writing with it on the darkness.

That night Ruth lay beside me on the same bed I'd been straining on all afternoon. The fresh sheets were fragrant and stiff, and occasionally Ruth would lift the top sheet so it billowed, stirring the air as it settled slowly back into place with a soft crumpling sound.

"I'm sorry," Ruth was saying in a low, earnest voice. "I just blurt things out sometimes without thinking. I'm not even sure it *was* a girl— I don't think you can really tell this early—"

I didn't say anything. My sinuses were swollen from crying and I was using my mouth to breathe.

"Becky?"

"It's all right," I said. "It doesn't matter anymore."

"It matters if you let it," Ruth said. "In something like this, if you let your feelings take charge you're lost—"

"Then I guess I must be saved," I said. "Because right now I just feel numb."

"Oh, Becky, I'm so sorry," Ruth was saying, and it was as if she hadn't heard me, as if she were talking to herself. "I'm not even sure it was a girl—it might've been a boy, you can't really tell—oh, God," she said, and then I could feel the bed start to tremble.

I reached over and held her hand. "Shhh," I said. "Shhh. . . ." I was lying on my back looking up at the ceiling. "Don't even think about it," I said. "Just pretend it never happened." Ruth was squeezing my hand. Underneath me the bed went on trembling, but I felt perfectly calm, as removed from all of this as a bloodless angel is from the tempests of the sea.

The next morning Ruth put on a cheerful face and tried to pretend that everything was back to normal. She said she wanted to pay a courtesy call on Reuben Benjamin to thank him for his help. They hadn't actually seen each other for years. He turned out to be a very tall, frail-looking old man with grizzled white hair and antique, wire spectacles. He lived in a new high-rise apartment with a view of the Schuylkill, and he received us in a three-piece suit that hung down from his shoulders without actually seeming to touch the body inside of it. While he and Ruth talked and drank coffee, I looked out the window at two needlelike sculls gliding down the river. Every time the oars touched the water, there'd be a tiny glint of silver. Dr. Benjamin was so long and thin he reminded me of some kind of water strider himself, or maybe a dragonfly. His gaze drilled right into you and seemed to search out everything there was to know. Just before Ruth and I left, while the three of us were standing at the door, he tilted my chin up with his finger and looked down into my eyes for a long moment. Then he began nodding his head as if he'd found what he was looking for. "You going to be all right," he told me. "Just fine. You going to have a long way to go, Rebecca, but I can see that you are a traveler." I wasn't sure what he meant, but I felt greatly reassured.

Two days later, though, when we got back home, the first thing I found out was that Robby Dodd had joined the Marines. I thought it was a sweet thing to do at first—an act of pure romantic ardor, like joining the Foreign Legion. But then, even before I left for college, he was off to boot camp, and the actuality of what he'd done finally began to sink in. To keep from feeling guilty, I wrote him faithfully throughout my freshman year, but in the spring—at about the same time my father was transferred to Edgewood Arsenal, in Maryland—Robby Dodd was shipped to Vietnam. The next fall I changed colleges, and after that, what with one thing and another, we completely lost touch. Sometimes I thought of him over there fighting in Vietnam, but I could never imagine Robby Dodd actually killing anybody. Whenever they showed newsclips of the war on TV, I always looked for him—but without ever having any luck.

Once, though, I did see a girl who looked like Sarah Williams. It was the fall of my senior year in college and I was living in Evanston,

Illinois. The abortion had become something I never consciously thought about anymore—I'd completely put it behind me. Then one evening around dusk I was sitting at a stoplight on Lake Shore Drive, and there was Sarah Williams staring at me from the back window of a Trailways bus. The glass was tinted and I couldn't tell for sure if it was really her. I followed the bus for a long way past my destination, trying as hard as I could to get a better look. But after a while it got too dark to see and I pulled the car over to the side of the road and turned the engine off. Ahead of me, the bus's taillights kept receding through one intersection after another, finally blending into the general flow of traffic until I lost them altogether. Cars were streaming by, their headlights wheeling past me, the white, whishing noise of their passing coming and going like a pulse, and I just sat there with my hand on the ignition, holding my breath and waiting to find out what it was I might be feeling, poised like that for a long time, right there on the verge.

Acknowledgments

I want to thank a number of people who contributed to this book. Doris Grumbach, George Core, and Gail Ross not only encouraged me, they were also instrumental in helping to publish my work. Bobbi Whalen, James Finnegan, Stephen Matanle, Sarah Wadsworth, Robbie Murphy, Laura Tracy, Maxine Clair, Judith Bowles, Faith Gussack, Candy Carter, and Barbara Goldberg each read draft after draft of these stories and worked hard to show me where I was going. Seymour and Manya Gussack, and The American University, where I teach, made it possible for me to take the extended time I needed. Finally, my wife, Amy Gussack, gave me not only the benefit of her clear-eyed editorial judgment but also the enabling support of her belief.

ILLINOIS SHORT FICTION